Greek Island Myst...

(Stand-alone thri...

Death

Of A Bride

By Luke Christodoulou

ALL RIGHTS RESERVED

Published by: G.I.M.

Edited by: Carol Tietsworth

Cover design: Maria Nicolaou (Mj.Vass)

Dedicated to the doctors and personnel of the Neonatal Intensive Care Unit of Macario Hospital for bringing my baby boy to life. You are life's true heroes.

Books by Luke Christodoulou:

The Olympus Killer (Greek Island Mystery #1) - 2014

The Church Murders (Greek Island Mystery #2) - 2015

24 Modernized Aesop Fables - 2015

Death Of A Bride (Greek Island Mystery #3) - 2016

Murder On Display (Greek Island Mystery #4) - 2017

Hotel Murder (Greek Island Mystery #5) - 2018

Twelve Months of Murder (Greek Island Mystery #6) - 2019

Beware of Greeks Bearing Gifts - 2020

Praise for the Greek Island Mysteries (Book Series):

All books in the series are rated 4-plus stars on Amazon, Goodreads and Book Reviewing Blogs.

'The Church Murders would appeal to any reader who enjoys murder mysteries, suspenseful reads, or action adventure novels. I am pleased to recommend this book and hope that author Christodoulou is working on his next book in this promising series.'

- Chris Fischer for Readers' Favorite

'The Greek James Patterson strikes again'

- Greek Media

'... does a masterful job writing a twisted murder story set under the Greek sun.'

- Ruth Rowley

'Greece is proud to have such a masterful author. Death of a Bride is his best offering by far.'

- Athens Review Of Books

'Superb murder/mystery. An Agatha Christie tale set in the 21st century.'

- National Society of the Greek Authors

'Great entertainment that begs to be made into a movie (...) a wealth of great stories here, well-paced and filled with believable characters, beautiful Greek imagery, fascinating insights into Greek culture and some wonderful, humorous touches.Excellent plot twists too - I really didn't see those coming. These stories can rival the bestsellers and - to be honest - the book knocks many of the famous names out of the park - an easy style, intense plot-lines, superbly lifelike characters and all this against the backdrop of gorgeous Greece and its fascinating history and culture.'

- Meandthemutts Book Reviewer

'The Church Murders is a juxtaposition of the beautiful (and gorgeously described) Greek Isles and the brutal, horrific murders that take place there'.

- Michael Young History

'Another one, I could not put down' – Jan Felton

'... meticulously crafted work. The author delivers another unique, powerful and provocative story'.

- Alex (Amazon Reviewer)

'Anxiously waiting for the next instalment!' - Jimmy Andrea (Amazon Reviewer)

'A spell-bounding thriller'. - Daniel T.A. (Author)

'As seductive as a Sudoku puzzle, the writer has crafted an ingenious plot with nothing less than stunning revelations at the conclusion.'

- Julius Salisbury (Author)

'If you like murder mysteries with great characters, atmospheric locations and a suspenseful, interesting plot to keep you turning the pages, then this book has been written for you'. –Ben (Amazon Reviewer)

'An engrossing murder mystery about a series of murders taking place on Greek islands.'

- Saritha S (Goodreads Book Reviewer)

'A tale of Terror! A page turning murder mystery'.

- Sheri A. Wilkinson (Book Reviewer)

'The author builds the main characters weaving them seamlessly with the plotting of a great story; even when he steps away from the present day mayhem. It's art in words at the highest pinnacle of a writer's work'.

- Rose Margaret Phillips (Book Blog Reviewer)

Chapter 1

Of all the plans a bride makes for her wedding day, dying is definitely not one of them.

Cassandra Zampetaki crept out of her family's mansion and dashed through the pouring rain, past the thrashing swimming pool and into the safety of the stone brick pool house. She quickly closed the glass door behind her, gasping to catch her breath. Blustery winds roamed the hilltop and fat drops of water crashed down mightily from the night sky. Nothing outside could compare with the storm inside Cassandra. Tomorrow she would walk down the aisle and become Mrs Cassandra Cara-Zampetaki. Her mother had insisted she keep her last name.

'It's a name with history behind it. What is a 'Cara'? A barbarian name...'

'Mother!' Cassandra would interrupt her and shoot a disapproving stare towards her.

Cassandra pulled the thick, vermilion curtains closed and turned on the lights. The expensive handcrafted chandelier came to life and pushed shadows back into corners. Cassandra ran her hands through her long, copper hair. She squeezed out as much water as she could and let it fall to the cold floor. She tied her hair up in a bun and stripped down to her underwear. Her fingers played with her gold engagement ring. It had been in Homer's family for five generations and she felt proud to have it gracing her hand.

With her heartbeat thrumming, she opened the doors of the heavy, wooden wardrobe and with a slight smile, she gazed at her wedding dress. She did not know why she felt compelled, but she had to try it on, just one more time before the *big day*. She struggled to wear it on her own and soon the silk, white Valentino dress settled on her curvy figure. She tiptoed to the wall mirror and twirled in delight.

As she spun, her eye caught a glimpse of a shadowed figure sitting behind her in the corner of the room. Her hand instinctively covered her faint scream as she tripped and fell to the tiled floor. The shadowy figure rolled her wheelchair into the light.

'Oh, it's you,' Cassandra said and exhaled deeply, obvious relief spreading across her diamond shape face. 'You gave me such a fright. What are you doing here?' Her voice climbed the decibel scale, going from abject nervousness to slight anger.

'I came here in the evening to enjoy the sunset over the cliffs and when the storm grew stronger and stronger, I decided to stay here,' the old lady said.

'Oh, Mrs Lakioti, why didn't you call up to the house?' Cassandra thought of the evening feast the woman had missed out on. No one had noticed her missing. She had been alone for hours.

'Now that is what I call a wedding dress. You look like an angel, my dear.'

'Thank you.' Cassandra turned back around and stared into the mirror. 'It was love at first sight. I knew this was *the* dress from the moment the saleslady carried it out. Of course, mother found it too plain...' Cassandra chattered away. Her flow of words covered the sound of stealthy footsteps behind her. The knife came down hard and sliced into her back. The acute, agonizing pain brought Cassandra to her knees. Before shock settled, the blade was yanked out of her fake-tanned skin. Cassandra screamed, only to be silenced by a second stabbing; this time straight into her throat. Blood sprayed onto the mirror and ran down the white dress, coloring it crimson red on its way down. The bride fell forward, eyes wide open, hands desperately seeking something to grasp. Outside, the storm grew even more violent; constant thunder broke through the air and howling, gale force winds uprooted old trees, while rain pummelled the grooved roof. Inside, Cassandra's last breath departed from her trembling lips and her body glided down the glass surface.

Her killer stepped into the pool of blood forming under her wedding dress. Garden cutters approached Cassandra's ring finger and with force, her murderer cut through the bone.

Chapter 2

Three weeks ago

'Costa, get up! And turn that hell-sent alarm clock off,' my lovely-after-her-morning-coffee wife moaned.

My eyes struggled to open and my hand clumsily searched for my alarm ringing cell phone amongst my pile of sci-fi books. *I really need to switch to Kindle, soon.* I slammed my hand down, offering silence to our warm bedroom.

'Shit, I'm late,' I said, realizing the time.

'Yes, I know. It's the third time that damn thing has woken me up. You kept on pressing snooze.'

I jumped out of bed and rushed into the bathroom. 'Going to get up and have breakfast?' I shouted to Tracy as I scratched my aching back and peed out last night's Tennessee whiskey.

'No way! It's my day off and I'm planning on going back to sleep. Now, stop talking to me and close the door.'

'Lucky you,' I replied, got dressed in a hurry, laid a kiss upon her warm cheek and sprinted out the door.

Root canal procedure. Stepping on Lego bricks while barefoot. Morning traffic in Athens. All inevitable evils of life.

I rolled down my Audi's front passenger windows and enjoyed the slight, November breeze. I accepted the fact that I was going to be late for work and relaxed amid in the chaos of honks and curse words that polluted the air. Thirty-five minutes later, I had parked in the underground parking of police headquarters. The air that hung between the grey, concrete walls was stale and thick with cigarette smoke lingering amongst it. Ever since administration banned smoking inside the police cafeteria, the parking and the roof became everyone's new hot spot.

I waved good morning to other officers on their way out for the morning's second coffee and third cigarette –all while their card had been punched in, of course.

The newly installed elevator carried me up to the fifth floor. I opened my brown briefcase and took out a few solved case files. I walked down the long corridor -that passed by fellow homicide Lieutenant's and Captain's offices- acting busy, ducked down into my papers, pretending to be reading them.

I am not late, I am busy.

I finally reached my office's glass door, grabbed the cool handle with my sweaty palm and with relief of not bumping into the grumpy, I-hate-people-being-late chief, I entered the two-desk room. Cherry scented air welcomed me. Ioli had already lit her candles. She disliked the smell of confined, office air.

Ioli looked up from her computer screen and grinned.

'Well, look at the party animal coming in late.'

'Shut up.'

'Good morning to you too, boss.'

'You look... fresh. I mean after all those drinks I saw you gulp down.'

She flashed her trademark smile. 'First of all, I did not realize you were going to chaperone me at your wife's birthday party. Second, I am a Cretan. We never get drunk. Third, most drinks were just orange juice. It's a defense mechanism. Keeps me busy, instead of looking like a Parthenon pillar. I can't dance to save my life. You on the other hand, burned the dance floor after consuming a month's supply of Jack.'

I rubbed my forehead. 'Don't remind me.'

'Midlife crisis getting worse?'

'Screw you!' I threw my head back and laughed. 'I was just happy to see Tracy having fun. And having friends! She doesn't say it or show it, but it hasn't been easy moving to Greece from New York. Actually, it was really the first time we both had fun since Gaby's death.'

Ioli's face darkened. 'I can't imagine how it must feel to lose a child...'

'There's no getting used to it or moving on or accepting it as part of life. You just keep living with a part of you missing.'

Awkward silence filled the room. Ioli was not only my partner; she was my best friend. However, too much honesty is not always a good thing. It was too early in the morning for such a depressing, *downer* conversation.

'What time did you leave the party?' I asked, redirecting the conversation back to the previous night.

'Around midnight. Cinderella had to get back to her parents.'

'I forgot that they are visiting. How's that working out?'

'Horrible. I love my parents, but they've been here three days now and I am suffocating. Mama keeps cooking and cleaning and Papa keeps asking when am I planning on getting married and offering him grandchildren. He keeps saying his heart won't last too long and going on about how the doctors said he should take it easy and enjoy his golden years with family. Hell, I tell you, hell. They want to see you, by the way. Their daughter's Savior.'

'I wouldn't call me that...'

'Well, they do. They even want to invite you to my cousin's wedding next month. Both you and Tracy. My whole family is dying to meet you.'

'Wedding? We don't even know the bride or groom...'

Ioli burst out laughing. 'In so many ways, you are still so freakin' American. Half the people at Greek weddings don't know the couple. Parents and the family invite most of the guests. Anyway, mama said it would be a nice vacation for us all and it's her way of re-paying you, Greek-style. She will house you and feed you. I'm the one who is going to have the hardest time, listening to how my aunts are all marrying off their younger-than-me offspring and Giannis's and Anna's thirty-five year old, only child is a homicide cop living alone in Athens.'

'Is the wedding in Chania?'

'No. In Gavdos.'

'Where? Is that a small Cretan village, I have never heard of?'

'It's an island actually. Only geography nerds and nudist know its existence.'

'You are a weird one, Cara. Why would only geography nerds and nudist know its existence?'

'Here, let me show you.' She swung round her computer screen and typed in Gavdos. Images of a small, triangular dot below Crete appeared in the first row of pictures. A caption read: THE MOST SOUTHERN POINT OF EUROPE. Deserted beaches with the sign NUDIST PARADISE, followed.

'Please tell me, it's not a nude wedding.'

'Stop making me laugh. Of course not, it's winter next month and freezing cold winds roam the island. Men would never agree to it.' Her laughter made it difficult to hear all her words clearly. 'The bride is from there. The wedding will take place at her mother's mansion. Her family is the richest family on the island, out of all sixty inhabitants.'

'That few?'

'Probably fewer in the winter. Until recently, the island did not even have electricity. Everything worked with generators.'

'Sounds lovely.' I raise my thick eyebrows and looked away.

'Don't be sarcastic. We'll have a great time. I don't want to go alone anyway.'

'Need a chaperone again?'

'I need a boyfriend to be honest. Someone to show off to my evil cousins and aunts and then dump the next day.' She fixed her high ponytail and turned back to her computer.

'Why dump him?' I dared to ask.

'Last thing on my mind...'

'So you say, so you say...'

I fell into my white, leather desk chair and stared at the phone. I needed a good case to wake me up.

Chapter 3

Two days before the wedding

My phobia of planes *–yes, I have finally accepted it as a phobia–* has made me a seafaring man. But, even I was unprepared for the storm forming before us. The Greek, postcard perfect, cyan sky darkened into a gravel grey. Soon, the turning to charcoal sky gathered black clouds above us. Aeolus, the Greek god of winds, was having a field day, unleashing his menacing winds all around us. The waves churned and swayed the steel, 200-yard ship. The vast, dark sea made the immense cruise ship seem insignificant, powerless even.

'Why didn't we just take the plane?' Gianni Cara, Ioli's father, complained as he sat, uneasy, on a stiffly uncomfortable lounge sofa, hand upon his stomach.

'Ssh, Gianni,' his wife, Anna, whispered. 'Costa is afraid of planes.'

'What? A tall, grown, muscular man like him? Ridiculous.'

I must admit, I was more pleased overhearing that I was considered muscular than offended. Last time I entered a gym, Freddie Mercury was still rocking the world.

Ioli's parents were just over a decade older than me, so around sixty, but looked much older. Working the land your whole life under the Greek sun has that effect. Both with white hair and deep, crow's feet lines around their eyes, but with kind, lively eyes and a genuine, Greek island smile. I watched as Gianni's thick and well-trimmed mustache jounced wildly as he complained about the eight hour journey from Peiraeus Port to Souda Port, near Chania.

'I'm sure we are going slower because of the high winds. It will take us twelve hours to get there.'

Sea water splashed against the round porthole that served as windows, making quite a few passengers jump and exchange worried looks at each other.

'I'm sorry, sir, for choosing...'

'Nonsense,' Ioli interrupted. 'Gianni loved the idea of taking the ship when he heard it was half the price.'

'Ioli always knew how to shut her father up,' Anna whispered to Tracy, who sat beside her, pale and motionless, in an effort to keep her egg and bacon breakfast in. Tracy forced a toothless smile. Her doleful face, stood out pale amongst her auburn, silk hair.

'Why the hell are we going to go to Gavdos in this weather? Stupid date for a wedding, if you ask me,' Gianni shifted his rant.

'Well, no one did ask you,' his wife finally spoke up. 'People do get married in the winter.'

'Not during a storm, on an isolated island reachable only by boat.'

'Maybe, it won't be as bad tomorrow,' optimist Anna said and placed her hand upon her husband's. Their love was obvious, deep, meaningful and after forty years of marriage still fresh. It brought shame to modern, shallow relationships. My own relationship with Tracy had so many ups and downs it could be a circus trampoline act.

As with all bad situations in life, the storm finally passed. Black clouds departed from the evening sky and the day's last rays journeyed down, a majestic shade of golden brown. Nothing is as beautiful as a winter sunset. Much calmer and quite relieved, passengers of Minoan Cruise Ship disembarked. A dull green bus awaited most, but not us.

'Ioli? Aunt Anna?' a deep, husky voice called over.

'I'd recognize that sexy voice anywhere. Homer!' Ioli shouted and ran into the tall man's long arms.

'Well, well, well. The groom himself, coming to pick us up. It is an honor,' Gianni joked and effortlessly carried his family's luggage to the dented, mud-covered pickup truck behind the chisel-faced young man.

'My God, you've grown all adult. Last time I saw you, you were just out of law school and then off to America.'

'Has it really been that long? Shame on us. Looking good, by the way,' Homer said and swirled Ioli around ala ballet style.

'You have to meet my friends. Costa lived most of his life in New York and his lovely wife, Tracy, is an American. Homer lives in Chicago,' Ioli said, turning towards us.

Homer extended his hand. He had a firm grip; my way of judging a man.

Tracy found the strength to shake off her drowsiness and talked about Chicago with Homer, while I –not so effortlessly- placed Tracy's 'all-necessary' luggage in the back of the 'does-this-still-run?' nineties truck.

'I love the name Homer,' Tracy said. 'There is something so Greek about it.'

'Really?' Homer said, and chuckled. 'Whenever I introduce myself back in the states, people normally go *duh!*'

'Guess we live in a world where the Simpsons are more famous than the Iliad.'

'To be honest, I prefer the Simpsons to the Iliad,' Homer joked and under the disapproving eye of his uncle, he rushed to unlock his vehicle.

Five foot Gianni rode shotgun, so six-foot-plus I had to squeeze into the back with Anna, Tracy and Ioli. I never knew my long, tree-trunk legs could bend that way.

'Your balls okay, babes?' Tracy whispered in my ear as she placed her right leg up on mine.

I chuckled and whispered back. 'Maybe you will have to check them afterwards.'

I looked over with envy at Ioli enjoying her space behind her rather short father while regretting sitting behind tall-as-me Homer. My knees could feel his heavy back, the leather chair creaked against my knees and suddenly a sense of claustrophobia kicked in. Without thinking, I rolled down the window in search of fresh air and the strong winds outside furiously invaded the confined space.

'What the...' Gianni turned around.

'Mmm, I love the smell in the air after a good downpour. So pure and fresh,' Anna cut him off.

'You know, there is a word for it. And it's based on ancient Greek of course,' Homer proudly announced, as I quickly rolled the window back up. 'Petrichor. From the words petra (stone) and ichor, the fluid that runs through the veins of the Olympian Gods.'

'I see you are still Mr Encyclopedia,' Ioli mocked him.

'That's nothing. I could have mentioned how the smell is really from bacteria in the earth, coming out of the soil as it is kicked up by the rain or analyze how the oxygen in the ozone...'

'La, la, la... please stop!' Ioli uttered the words between squeaky laughing sounds.

'Twenty years later and you two are still acting like kids,' Gianni said, but I could not tell if he was joking or being serious. I had a feeling it swung more towards the latter.

The timid winter sun was falling to the west, sinking into a stormy horizon. More rain was heading our way. As the last sun rays vanished from the serene, blue sky, we entered the picturesque town of Chania, Ioli's home town. Homer took the scenic route and soon the magical aura of the Venetian harbor surrounded us.

'It's so beautiful,' Tracy said. It was her first time in Crete. 'No, beautiful is too small. It's magnificent,' she continued.

I could see all four Cretans gloat. There were proud islanders. *As if there is any other kind?*

Arabs, Turks, Egyptians and Venetians all made a pass from the island on the rising of their empires and left when they fell. All had left their mark on the landscape. Unique buildings blended together to create architectural marvels. As if a cultural, architectural festival had been held and participates from all over competed and left their buildings behind. A Venetian fort was on one side, a gracious mosque on the other. Cretan houses next to Arabic mansions. A sense of living history lingered in the air. That and the smell of meat being cooked for kebabs ready-to-go. Thankfully, my belly –though empty- refrained from ruining the silence with its usual, loud, crocodile-resembling rumbles.

Very few people could be seen walking down the narrow streets, and most of the souvenir shops and tavernas seemed closed.

'This is how you know the best places to eat,' Ioli said. 'They stay open in the winter as they serve locals, too. The *tourist* places take the winter off.'

The light from the grand, stone lighthouse swooped through the night sky and flashed right through the car, revealing angry waves crashing over the mouldy stone walls below.

'In my tour guide...'

You could take Tracy for a day trip to a nearby village and she would still buy a tour book or search the internet for things to do and sights to see. She believed in being informed.

'... it had a line that I loved about Chania. A rural town, with the comforts of a city and the beauties of a developed village.'

We said goodbye to the ocean and turned into town. The fluorescent street lights were too weak to fight off the invading darkness that surrounded them. Clouds blocked out the stars and the crescent moon. Lightning forced through the dark clouds and cracked the night sky, shining light above the gothic arch to our left.

'This is the entrance to the archaeological museum...' Gianni paused his tour to let thunder run its course. '... It used to be a Franciscan monastery up until the sixties. I used to love coming here for school trips,' history buff Gianni continued. 'You can see the whole history of the island. The blend of cultures. Minoan artifacts upon a Roman era mosaic floor, Arabic spears and swords against Venetian walls...'

'Dogs humping,' Ioli added, and we all –Homer included-mindlessly turned to see the two shabby strays in front of the empty, dilapidated building next to the museum.

The penetrating honking and slamming of the brakes that followed sent shivers down my aching back. Tracy squeezed my hand while Ioli did what she did best. Cursed.

The car swerved and climbed up the pavement before coming to a complete stop.

The cab with which we nearly crashed, did not bother to stop. It slowed down just enough for us to notice a big-bellied taxi driver flip us the finger and call Homer a *malaka*. However, the passengers in the back were those that caught my attention.

A well-groomed, forty-something year old bearded man sat next to a black-haired lady who arched two manicured eyebrows at us. Patches of bruises covered her face. The skin on her face looked like it was ripped and then sewed on by my three year old niece. Deep, maroon lines ran freely around her eyes and nose, and all the way down to her neck. You could not distinguish her lips amongst the severe, bloody blisters that covered the lower part of her face.

'I'm so sorry,' Homer rushed to apologize.

'No need to apologize. It's my daughter's fascination with dog *humping* that is to blame.'

'Thanks, dad. Good to know,' Ioli replied.

The rest of the twenty-minute drive went by rather uneventfully. We sat tranquilly as the sky wore its charcoal coat and ominous, black clouds gathered and blocked out the stars.

'Home, sweet home.' Anna's cheerful voice was the first to break the silence.

The old truck turned down the muddy, dirt road and won a bumpy fight to reach the two story farm house.

The rumbling in the skies above warned us to hurry into the house. One numb leg after another, I exited the vehicle. I felt a weird pain in my stomach as I tried to stand up straight. *First my back, now this... and next year I'm hitting the big 5-0...*

'Costa, quick,' Tracy's voice pulled me back to reality. The first drops of rain lazily fell as if out for a stroll. Everyone took a piece or two of luggage and sprinted into the house.

An hour later, with warm, sour frumenty soup resting well in our stomachs, we said our goodnights. Homer left for his family home – two farms down- and not long after, snoring and heavy breathing ruled the century-old house.

It turned out that roosters did not need light to know it was dawn. The animal's ferocious cry came at six o'clock sharp. I slowly rose and stumbled to the wooden-framed window. Outside, a pitch black sky cried down thin droplets. The tin roofs of pig and cow sheds danced with spray. Sunlight was nowhere to be seen.

I awoke Tracy with a kiss on her rosy cheek –*I could never understand how she remained so warm through the cold night, I awoke a popsicle, like always*- and opened the oak wood door, letting in the sweet aroma of the Greek coffee brewing in the kitchen down below. Anna apparently beat the rooster on most mornings.

A thick wood, country table filled with nature's finest breakfast awaited us. Home-made feta cheese graced with pure, Cretan olive oil, three kinds of olives and freshly cut, chopped tomatoes and cucumbers were lined up beside Anna's home-baked bread. Time had reached the fifties in Anna's kitchen and has since stood still.

'Eat up quickly,' Gianni grunted, as we sat down. 'The bus leaves in an hour. Homer will be here to pick us up soon.'

'People tend to say good morning first,' Ioli said, with a smile towards us. She kissed her father tenderly on the side of his forehead and then sat down beside him.

Unlike a typical Greek, Homer came on time. *Great. More time squeezed in the back seat.*

Luckily for my knees and most of the boned joints in my body, the bus station lay only a ten minute drive away. Homer's dated, dented truck fought against muddy puddles forming speedily along the gravel road. Asphalt road came as a blessing to our tossed around stomachs.

The rain grew stronger, hammering against the aluminium kiosk where we ran to take cover and pay for our tickets.

I took out my wallet and Ioli's eyes widened. 'Don't you dare! It's on me. I invited you, Cretan hospitality and all.'

I tried to protest, but then remembered mama's 'golden rule'. Never argue with a Greek woman when her mind has been made up.

Drains were already overflowing, a sign of lazy council workers who only cleaned out the sewer if and when the situation had reached a point of no return.

We dashed through the rain and into the small, yet sufficient bus station building. There, the Cara family had assembled and loud chatter filled the low ceilinged room. Loud good mornings and even louder kisses were exchanged and introductions were rapidly made.

'You and your elephant memory will have to help me remember everybody's name,' Tracy whispered in my ear as a barrel-chested man squeezed my hand.

'And this is my uncle Thomas and his wife Georgia...' Ioli continued with the ongoing introductions as two young boys ran around us, using us as a barrier in their shooting games. Ioli suddenly paused and stood still. Her gaze focused on the athletic, tall, handsome, olive skinned man approaching her with a smile as vast as the Pacific. His 'James Franco' green eyes were fixed steadily on her.

'Hi, Ioli,' he said, stopping his fast pace just a foot away from her.

'Get the fuck out of here. It can't be.'

'You always had a way with words,' he said. His tongue gently wet his lips and he flashed an awkward smile.

'Mark? Oh my God. I can't believe this. How have you been?' Ioli hugged him, placing her chin on his broad left shoulder. It was the first time, I saw her hug anyone besides her parents. Not one for much *social touching*.

'A detective, not informed? I'm the best man.'

'You're shitting me. How do you...'

'I studied in America. Met Homer on our first day at Uni at an unspeakably corny Greek welcoming event. As if we went to America to hang around with other Greeks all day.'

'And after all those years of university, Homer ended up with a Greek girl and a Greek best man.'

He laughed a heavy, genuine, manly laugh. 'You do have a point.'

'So, where is your Greek girl?'

His smile reached his somewhat pointy ears. 'No girl. Just me. No time for commitments at med school.'

'You're a doctor?'

'Surgeon,' he monolectically replied, trying not to sound pompous but still hoping to impress. 'You?'

'Me, what?' Her left-hand thumb ran along her sharp, red nails; her right hand casually pushed back a few black hairs on the loose, neatly tucking them behind her ear.

'Where's your guy?' Mark asked, leaning slightly forward.

'Are we really doing this?'

'Doing what?'

'The whole *I'm single, I'm single, too* situation?'

His smile grew too large for his face. 'So, you are single? I'll keep that in mind.'

'Well, look at little Mark, all grown up and flirting at weddings.'

His smile flat-lined for a second, before the tips of his lips rose again. 'I...'

'.. Hate being called little Mark. I know, I know. I must have heard you complain a million times,' Ioli interrupted.

'Hey, it wasn't easy being the smallest kid in class.'

Only then, did Ioli –and Mark for that matter- realize that Tracy and I were standing next to them the whole time. We had faded into the background of the crowded room.

'Oh, Mark, this is my partner Costa and his wife Tracy. This is...'

'Mark. We heard,' I said with a grin, only to receive a *watch-it* look from Ioli. She received my 'what-did-I-say', oblivious look, in return.

'Pleasure to meet you,' Tracy said, extending her hand.

'Old friends, I guess?' I asked.

'We were classmates for five years at primary school, but then my family moved to Athens and we haven't seen each other since.'

'Bus is here, everyone!' Homer shouted over the loud group. He herded us through the glass doors and counted us as we boarded the dated, 'begging-for-a-wash' vehicle. It was a regular field trip.

The engine roared to life and Kazantzakis's old hits blasted through the badly-wired, crackling speakers.

I had seen many roads in the nearly five decades that I have roamed this planet and the long, winding, 'next-to-certain-death-cliffs' mountain road we were on, was not a road. It was a roller coaster ride designed in hell by the man in charge himself. We journeyed with speed close to rugged cliffs and with horror watched our 'got-my-license-during-WWII' driver, talk on his phone, while smoking a pack of Assos cigarettes and scratching all over, while he drove.

The Cretan passengers were oblivious to the mayhem. Greek clichés came alive as women exchanged recipes and talked about their offspring, while the men discussed sports and the new prime-minister. Ioli sat behind us, alone and quiet, gazing towards the vast horizon. Wild nature welcomed the drops of water that free-fell through the sky and splattered against the muddy grounds.

'Are your sea legs ready for the boat ride to the island?' I placed my head against Tracy's.

'Don't remind me.' Her hand fell upon my knee. 'Just love me and pay attention to me, these days.'

'Don't I always?'

'We have both been so busy lately. This get-away could not have come at a better time.'

We said no more. Shouting interrupted our little moment. The on-going discussion on politics quickly heated and reached boiling point. Just like every discussion on politics in Greece.

'I wish he had the guts to leave the Euro zone!' Gianni said angrily.

'I wish old people like you really understood what a disaster that would truly be!' Jason, Homer's younger brother, replied.

'Who you calling old, you little piece of...?'

'And I wish for a mute supermodel that enjoys cooking and cleaning,' Thomas, Ioli's uncle, said. Laughter from all drove the argument right out the wet, trembling bus windows. The wind grew stronger, the rain fell heavier and Paleochora -where our boat waited for us finally appeared on the horizon. It lay peacefully by the wavy, deep blue sea. Our ferry teetered upon the hostile waters. Ioli read Tracy's look.

'It takes less than an hour to reach the island. By the time we gossip about the bride's side, we'll have arrived,' Ioli joked, receiving a wide smile from my wife.

'The bride's side?' I asked.

'Yes, her guests have been staying at her mansion since yesterday. There is only one ferry and it runs every morning. She has relatives and friends over from America as well. They arrived ...'

'Ioli, go help your mother,' Gianni ordered as the bus came to a complete halt.

'Only in Greece, you never truly grow up enough to not be told what to do by your parents,' Ioli said with a smile, and went off to help her mother unload bags of silverware and home-made food, presents for the bride's parents. We were staying at their mansion and as all Greeks know well, you must go all out with presents for your hosts.

The rain had taken a break; the high winds though, apparently had no such plans.

The picturesque, dark brown from the rain, wooden pier welcomed us. Everyone moved speedily, not trusting the threatening clouds releasing lightning and thunder above us.

'Zeus is surely in a mood today,' Homer joked, as he helped his parents to board. The metallic, narrow bridge swung side to side erratically; the passengers all calculating the right time to hop on.

'I always wanted to sign up for Wipe Out,' a loud woman's voice was heard. Her uproarious laughter sliced through the air. She wore a tight, red, glittery dress, dark shades, matching high heels, a dead, furry animal wrap and an air of confidence. Her date, a well-preserved forty year old –at least ten years her senior- followed; his body at one with the countless suitcases.

'Cousin Leonida,' Homer greeted him with a pat on the back.

'Kallisto,' he called ahead, bringing the diva to a standstill. 'Baby, this is the groom. My cousin, Homer. Homer, this is Kallisto...'

'Kallisto Ralli,' Homer said in admiration. 'I've never met anyone famous before.'

Kallisto extended her glove-wearing hand. 'Leonida, you failed to mention how handsome he was.' Homer turned a light shade of red.

'Genes, my dear. He's my cousin, you should have guessed,' Leonida joked and walked on; the burden of the luggage grew heavier.

'Famous?' I whispered to Ioli.

'She stars in Dysfunctional Housewives. Played quite a lot of theatre when she was in Greece. Never was the main star though.'

'Dysfunctional Housewives?' I could not help but laugh.

'A low-rated cable show in America, but she seems to believe she is a celebrity.'

The couple approaching caught my glance. A feeling of familiarity was born inside my overworked brain. *No way. The couple from the taxi!*

'Where is your A.D.D. mind drifting off to?' Ioli asked.

'The taxi we nearly hit today,' I murmured, and strolled off, acting casual, passing by the couple, overhearing Homer greet the man as cousin George. George then introduced his girlfriend Melissa. Homer showed no sign of paying any attention to her severely burnt face, unlike Kallisto, whose eyes lowered to their corners and her red lips twisted in disgust. She turned before any introductions could have been made.

'Quickly, Leonidas,' she ordered and paraded towards the ship.

Leonidas hugged his cousin, George, shook hands with Melissa and dawdled down the pier. A Greek man never shows that a woman bosses him around. When he was sure they we were not watching, he ran and boarded the bouncing boat, calling after his loved one.

The clouds laid low on the horizon, conspiring on tomorrow's attack. For the time being, they had retreated and blessed us with a clear sky.

'If the wind would only stop,' Tracy complained.

'If only,' Ioli agreed.

'Are George and Leonida your cousins too?'

'Huh?' Ioli said, unsure she heard right. She was expecting a mindless comment on the weather. 'Erm, no. Homer's dad and mine are brothers. They are from his mother's side of the family. How do you... You were snooping around down on the dock. I thought you needed to walk off your grandpa-back pain.'

'Don't call it that,' I said with a wide smile, enjoying Tracy's giggle.

'You really should have it checked out, Costa. It might not only be old age,' Tracy said, her giggle settling down. Now, it was Ioli's turn to laugh.

'You two are having a ball, aren't you?'

I received no response. With a loud roar, the ferry's engines came to life and Kallisto's high pitched voice competed with them to be heard.

'Did you get the keys to the cabin, Leo?'

'Yes, dear,' he replied. 'Here you are. I'm going to stay and see my aunts...'

'Do whatever pleases you,' she said with apathy, waving her hand. 'I need to lie down, in *peace*,' she emphasized. All the loud talking Cretans were working wonders on Kallisto's morning migraine. They went their separate ways, ignoring us sitting just feet away.

'A cabin? For an hour-something trip?' Tracy asked.

'Some people have too much money to waste,' Ioli replied.

The ferry picked up speed and water splashed over the rails. The waves were at war with the strong winds.

'I know you prefer fresh air, but shouldn't we be heading inside?' I asked my slightly pale wife.

'Yes, let's. I love Cretans when they gather. You never know what you are going to hear.'

'That's for sure,' Ioli said, standing up.

Inside, in a room born out the dark corners of a claustrophobic's mind, Aristo and Cleopatra Cara –Homer's parents- worked hard to meet everybody's needs. A bitter Greek coffee for Gianni, a sweet one for Jason and a lighter for Leonida who enjoyed a smoke with his cousin George, while his girlfriend, Melissa, sat behind him playing with her fingers and staring out to the ever-moving ocean. She could feel the eyes pretending not to see her.

'Poor thing,' Anna said. 'Imagine being on fire.' Her shoulders trembled at the idea.

'I heard she was in a car accident,' Georgia whispered back. 'The car caught fire and she was trapped inside.'

The boat's loud horn did not interrupt any of the on-going conversations.

'Nothing compared to galas back in New York?' Ioli joked, as we stood at the door.

'They do love talking, don't they?' Tracy laughed.

'Excuse me, can you help me?' a frail voice came from behind me as we entered the room. An old lady, in her early eighties, sat in her wheelchair, unable to force herself up the two-inch step that was blocking her entrance to the room.

'Of course,' I replied, and helped her in.

'Thank you, young man.'

'Hear that dear?' I called over to Tracy. 'Young man!' I said with a grin.

'Aunt Myrrine,' the ladies on the boat came close and surrounded her.

It was a scene taken out of a Greek fifties movie. You had your strong men, your gossiping women, a wedding on the way and now, the elderly aunt from America.

Time melted away like spring snow. Soon, the ferry became a distant memory and the Cara family, plus two, arrived at the Zampetaki mansion.

Chapter 4

The day before the wedding

'Holy fuck! This place is bigger than parliament,' Ioli gracefully said, as the bus entered through the freshly-painted gates of Zampetaki manor. Two lines of majestic palm trees ran alongside the road. Grass covered the majority of the vast farmland, while square patches of fine, black dirt indicated that the place truly came alive with flowers during spring. The taxi –or rather a local's old car that acted like one- that had brought the dysfunctional housewife and her luggage carrying boyfriend was already on its way out.

Gianni rolled his eyes and held back from shouting for the millionth time a *watch your language young lady* warning. He had given up. Defeated once more by Ioli's rich vocabulary.

'Will she ever learn?' he asked his wife.

Anna raised her hands. 'I try to believe, that God made her just the way he intended.'

'You sure it was God?' Gianni asked, smiling for the first time. A smile knocked off his face by Anna's right hand.

'Don't be silly,' she said, and slapped him on the back of his going-bald head.

The 19th century, twenty-bedroom country house towered us as we exited the bus.

'The walls of Troy with windows,' Thomas joked.

The sound of the heavy doors opening, gathered us into a half-cycle before its carved wooden facade. Bright light shone through the gap and out ran a young lady wearing faded jeans and a burgundy turtle neck. She ran straight into Homer's arms and kissed him with force on his dry lips. Everyone smiled at the couple. Everyone, that is, besides the bride's mother who stood by the door wearing a formal evening dress, white pearls and a bored expression. Her husband was more expressive. In his black suit he shook hands with everyone, introducing himself and ushering us into his home.

'I am Cosma Zampetaki, please come in out of the cold. This is my wife Irene. You might not be able to tell, but she is very pleased to meet you.'

The icy look from his wife competed with the cold winds as to who could freeze us first. 'This is my mother, Helena Zampetaki,' Cosma continued, ignoring his wife's mien. 'Age 91,' he proudly announced, hugging the fragile looking, black-wearing woman. Her white, silvered hair was escaping her black head scarf and whipping her wizened face. She smiled a friendly smile, though her eyes examined us thoroughly. A sample of the Greek hospitality blended with the suspicious mind of elders.

'And this is my wife-to-be, Cassandra,' Homer proudly announced lifting his fiancé up.

Inside, the Zampetaki family and friends gathered in the vast reception area with the two twirling stairways and the golden, hanging chandelier.

The introductions, the explanation of who was who and the exchange of gifts lasted longer than our journey to the isolated island. A quite stout lady in her late forties went around offering her hand and introducing herself as the bride's aunt. The bride's very bubbly and very colorful friends stood out like a farm fly in strained yogurt. Alexandra, Andrea, Jenny and Amanda tried hard to remember all the names they heard. The four single ladies were sure to remember Jason, who had kissed each one on the hand.

'Oh, to have young blood running through your veins,' lamented Aunt Myrrine.

Two patient, serious-looking butlers waited to escort us all to our rooms. The rest of the house's help was busy in the kitchen below, preparing the night's feast.

Soon, all settled into 1940's style bedrooms with thick, colorful carpets and the tall beds that you had to long jump or climb up if you wished to rest. Outside, lighting sliced the dark sky like a pitchfork through hay. Thunder shook the ground and ferocious winds carried the rain through the cold air. As the storm grew stronger, my eyelids grew weaker. A midday nap in the arms of my lover came as a treat after all the travelling. I set my alarm clock for six. One hour would be enough for Tracy to prepare for tonight's party at seven.

I always found it funny how clothes and make up -clothes and a good shave for the guys- could change a person. Every guest walked down the granite stairs all shiny and new. Diamonds cleared from the mud. Expensive jewels lay around necks and fingers while hair defied gravity and was formed into fashionable hairstyles. More importantly, all wore an aura of relaxation, a vibe of vacation, a feeling of *we are going to have a good time*.

The dining room doors opened and welcomed us into its stomach. And what a stomach it was.

'You could fit my apartment four times over into this room,' I whispered to Ioli. She looked stunning in her black silk dress.

'Sorry, I wasn't listening,' she joked, as she pointed to the mile long buffet table. 'I think I've died and gone to food heaven.'

Towers of porcelain plates stood at the beginning, a variety of Greek salads were next and every single food in a Greek cookbook followed. A scent of well-cooked meat lingered in the heated, thick air.

'I'm going to need more plates,' Ioli laughed.

'I'm taking an extra plate for the kontosouvli at the end,' Mark said and politely squeezed between us. Tracy double raised her eyebrows at me.

'I love watching people flirt,' she said, and her almond shaped eyes glowed with excitement.

'Then, just look at me baby,' I replied with the same grin that had graced my mischievous face since puberty.

Through the huge oval windows we witnessed the night sky fall like a curtain down to the dark sea. The storm rolled in strong; blaring music and Kallisto's riotous laughter covered the plethora of thunder served out by the night clouds.

Stories were told over wine and food and as the servants took away our dessert plates, the party escalated. Even I could not resist joining in on the on-going hasapiko on the dance floor. However, I did not risk going for a solo zempekiko, as I did not trust my back. Flowers were thrown around, bottles were smashed, people were shouting, smoking and singing; just another Greek party. I did not dare imagine the scope of wedding festivities the following night.

Slowly-slowly, one by one the guests thanked Cosma and Irene Zampetaki for their hospitality, wished them a long life and many grandchildren, and wobbled off to their rooms. The euphoria from all the fine wine and the tasty Cretan Raki having drawn wide smiles across their faces. By midnight, pretty early for a Greek feast, everyone had sailed off to dreamland. Tomorrow was the wedding. No one wished for a hangover or sleepiness.

Cassandra had kissed Homer good night and managed to resist joining him in his room.

'There will be plenty of time for that, lover boy.'

They kissed for some minutes, enjoying each other's lips, lost in a heavenly embrace. Heavy breathing departed their hot lips and hands travelled across their bodies. Cassandra pulled back, caught her breath, blew Homer a kiss and ran off to her room.

Homer stripped down to nothing. The central heating was set to satisfy the cold-bottomed grandparents. He jumped onto the soft bed, thanked God for Cassandra and in a matter of seconds his snoring filled the warm room.

Cassandra had no such luck. It was not a case of cold feet. It was pure excitement. She gazed out of her window; looking through the raindrops that splattered against it. She had hid her dress in the pool house. She had taken no chances of Homer seeing it.

'Screw it,' she said out loud after an inner pep talk. She quietly sneaked out of the room, slowly closing the heavy, screeching door.

Minutes later, the blade sliced through her throat. Her blood shot out high and her lifeless body fell to the ground.

The following morning, breakfast was served in the same grand style as last night's feast. But Aunt Myrrine and the bride to be were nowhere to be seen.

Irene Zampetaki was trying discreetly to tell-off the two maids for not having washed all the silverware yet.

'The guests are coming down to breakfast and you are telling me we haven't got enough knives and forks?'

'Madame, we used almost all of them last night. The dish washer could fit only so many...'

'Well, you should have stayed up last night and washed them by hand.'

'On it, right away, ma'am,' the skinny, young brunette said with eyes lowered to the floor. The second maid stayed.

'Yes?' Irene asked with apathy.

'We have an extra set in the pool house,' said the forty-something year old woman.

'Then, what are you waiting for?'

And just like that, the tall lady ran down to the kitchen, picked up a large, black umbrella and dashed out into the storm. The icy tiles by the empty pool made it difficult to walk. For a second, the rain stopped. Just before Katerina could thank the Lord for the reprieve, lighting tore the dark, ominous sky and thunder roared from behind tumultuous clouds. Katerina let out a weak scream as hail dived out of the ragged clouds and hit upon her umbrella forcibly. That inner force we humans possess at moments when we are in trouble came alive and Katerina moved with speed towards the hail-battered pool house. She leapt into the room, glad to be out of the storm. She was not glad to suddenly slip in a puddle of blood. She landed face first upon Cassandra's stabbed body; her arms helping her to stop inches away from the dead bride's face. Katerina shrieked in terror. As she tried to stand up without touching the body, her screams grew louder than the howling winds outside. She took a few unstable steps back and curled up in the room's corner. With trembling hands, she searched for her cell phone. Her apron hung from off her thin waist and dipped into the pool of blood. With eyes fixed resolutely on the ceiling, she pulled her phone out of the top left pocket of her white shirt. She could never stand the sight of blood. Her head leaned forward heavily. She felt like fainting. Shaky hands travelled across the phone's surface and managed to dial the house's number.

'Hello? Zampetaki residence,' Christina's formal voice came through the receiver.

'Christina, its Katerina.' Pause. She opened her mouth for air. 'I'm in the pool house...'

'Yes, I know. Madame is waiting for...'

'The bride is dead!' Katerina screamed.

An awkward silence was followed by disbelief. Reality kicked its way through the fog.

Christina left the house phone hanging, ran down the long hallway and zombie walked into the crowded breakfast room. She stood in the doorway and tried to speak louder than the jovial guests. The third time she spoke, all froze.

'What did you say?' Cosmas asked standing up.

'Miss Cassandra is dead in the pool house,' she said, and then she turned white and –under other circumstances- quite comically fell to the floor. The poor girl had fainted.

Chairs fell back as people leapt out of them. As one we all ran towards the door. Outside, Cosma, Irene, Homer, Ioli and I did not stop at the sight of the hail. The rest of the guests stayed beneath the safety of the wooden, bougainvillea-covered pergola. Eyes, wide open, followed us to the pool house. Hands covered mouths in shock upon hearing the manic screams of despair from the bride's parents. Homer fell to his knees and was going to take his beloved fiancée into his arms, only to be stopped by Ioli.

'Don't. Evidence,' she whispered two words, as she took Homer into her arms. His father Aristo entered the room to fall behind his son and hug him, too. Homer's mother Cleopatra saw the blood from the entrance and did not dare enter.

I knelt to the ground, too. A piece of paper floated in the puddle of blood.

'I am not your aunt Myrrine. My name is Maria Marousaki. Wife of Ioanni Marousaki. I have done my duty. I can now die in peace,' I read the note.

Irene had fallen to the floor and was screaming hysterically, while her husband paced up and down the room cursing and calling upon saints to save his little girl. Both were in a clear state of shock. At the sound of the surname Marousaki both froze. Tears fell silently. They gazed at each other for what seemed to be centuries. Ioli could not take the silence.

'Who is she?'

No reply. Irene slapped her husband hard across his face, and ran outside. The clouds had run out of hail and had gone back to leaking skinny drops of water. Irene walked steadily towards the cliff. She stood on the edge and stared down to the newly born river that cut through the ground, 120 feet below. She closed her eyes, whispered the little prayer her mother had taught her as a child and stepped forward.

Hands came out of nowhere and grabbed her by the waist, stopping her downward trajectory and forcing her to the muddy ground. Irene opened her eyes and tried to focus. A breathless Kallisto lay upon her.

Jason and Leonida arrived next. They had run from the house, having seen Irene approach the edge.

'God, you're fast,' Jason said, in admiration.

'And in high heels, too, kid,' Kallisto replied, standing up.

Leonida helped Irene to her feet.

'My daughter's dead. Dead. Let me fall, let me fall,' Irene cried until her husband picked her up and with the help of Leonida and George, carried her back to the house.

Ioli and I stood by the pool house. Rain bounced in muddy puddles and lighting flashed around us.

'Look,' Mark said, having run out of the house and straight towards Ioli.

Aunt Myrrine's wheelchair lay, knocked over in the mud, a foot from the edge.

'I can now rest in peace,' Ioli recalled the old lady's note. 'Do you think she jumped?'

'Looks like it. Or this is what this scene is supposed to look like,' I replied, lost in thought.

Everyone stood around, uncertain how to proceed next. Hail returned, forcing them back into the mansion.

'Mark,' I called over. 'You're a doctor, right?'

'Yes, sir.'

'Come in,' I said, rushing back into the pool house. Inside, Ioli was preoccupied with Myrrine's note.

Mark paused for a second at the sight of the girl's body before acting professionally and kneeling down beside her.

'I guess you want my opinion on time of death?'

'Clever lad,' I said and forced a flat line smile. There was something wrong with the sight of a dead young woman in her wedding dress. Sort of unnatural. Wedding days are a celebration of life, of union, of hopes of offspring, of continuing life.

'Can I touch her?' Mark asked, interrupting my 1000-word-a-minute producing mind.

'Wait a sec.' I looked around. I walked into the next room, turning on the lights. Outside, the black sky seemed to attack the earth with considerable force. I approached the lower kitchen cupboards and searched around, among insect repellent, washing up liquid and a bag of last summer's onions. I picked up the box of latex cleaning gloves, pulled out two pairs and returned to the one sofa, two armchairs, and one dead body room.

'Here.' I extended my hand, offering Mark a pair.

With care, we rolled over the body. Mark's eyes ping-pong from the girl's missing finger to my face.

'She stole her ring,' he said, his voice slightly screeching as it got louder.

Ioli looked over for a second, stared at the bride's hand, then her punctured throat and looked back down at the note.

I stood up, leaving Mark to examine the body.

'OK, I am curious. What's so fascinating about the note?'

Ioli passed me the note and asked, 'does this look like old lady's writing to you?'

'I remember my grandma's writing and how I hardly understood what she had written. I mean, what eighty-year old lady writes in Modern Greek? The monotonic orthography was introduced when I started school. Even my mother uses the polytonic system when it's for her own use. And not only that, look at the letters -all nice and tidy. You would expect an old lady's hand to shake a little, especially when she was planning on killing a girl and then committing suicide,' Ioli continued.

'You never seize to amaze me, Cara.'

'She always was one of a kind,' Mark said standing up. 'So, what do you think happened?' he asked.

She shrugged her shoulders and uncrossed her arms. 'At the moment, fuck knows. We are going to have to investigate this, but Mark, no one needs to know more details right now than they should. It's just a hunch, a suspicion. The worst thing at the moment would be to cause panic.'

Mark nodded in agreement as thunder shook the windows.

'Anything from the body?' I asked.

'Well, judging on the cold temperature and the puncture wounds, I would say she bled to death in a matter of minutes; sometime after midnight.'

'She left the party around that time. I remember her saying her good nights as we exited the room,' Ioli said. 'The old lady must have stood up to stab her in the neck,' she continued, murmuring to herself as she approached us.

We stood puzzled above the body.

'OK, here's the plan,' I spoke, breaking the silence. 'We go to the house, say that this is a crime scene and no one is to come near the pool house. You should call Chania Police Headquarters to send a coroner and forensic officers. I will interview her friends and Homer. Someone should know why she was down here, alone at night and if anyone had threatened to hurt her. The hard part will be interviewing her parents. They knew who the old lady really was. There's a back story there, for sure.'

Ioli and Mark ran through the downpour towards the house; dozens of worried eyes following them from behind the huge windows. I locked the pool house door and tucked the key away in my jacket's right pocket. My hands were cold and numb. The temperature had taken a dive since yesterday and today's storm made all others I had witnessed look insignificant.

Running through the hard falling rain, stepping on hail stones the size of a hazelnut and having fierce, freezing winds embrace you, was definitely not something my back or knees were up for. I accepted my defeat and stopped running. I walked the distance left towards the mansion's side door, entered the house exhausted and wet, and exhaled deeply, happy to be back into a roofed environment. I stood in the center of the carpet room, soaked through and through with water streaking down my face in rivulets, and raised my voice for all to hear.

'I am Captain Papacosta with the Hellenic Police. No one is to go near the pool house. No one is to leave this mansion without permission and without being interviewed. If anyone has any information about last night's events, this is the time to come forward.' I paused. I was circled by all the guests and house servants. Only the bride's parents were missing; they were upstairs in their bedroom. People stood by their loved ones and some even held hands. Anna had her head leaning against her strong husband. Watery eyes focused on me. A few silent tears travelled down cold cheeks. 'We will get to the bottom of all this. Please remain calm and cooperate with the police.'

That is when I noticed Ioli pacing up and down in the background. One hand held her phone to her ear, while the other waved angrily through the air.

'Thank you,' I said with a toothless smile and I turned to approach Ioli.

'What's wrong?' I asked as she lowered the phone.

'No ships are allowed to sail because of the storm. It is even worse above the sea. I called the chief and he said it's up to us to solve it.'

'Well, at least no can leave. If you are right and that note wasn't written by that old lady, then we have a murderer or an accomplice among us,' I whispered.

'I know most of the people here. I'll interview the guests and I think it is better you talk to the parents. You have your way with dealing with grieving people. I suck at it.'

'Is everything okay?' Tracy asked, her soft hand stroking my wet neck.

'Local police can't make it because of the storm. We are going to have to take on the case ourselves. Babe, sorry...'

'Don't be ridiculous, Costa. I know you're a good man, but for crying out loud, don't apologize for ruining our mini holiday. You didn't kill her.'

'I love this woman,' Ioli said, placing her hand on Tracy's shoulder and went to find Homer.

I kissed Tracy gently on her cheek. 'Go to our room, watch some trash morning TV. Don't stay down here with all these mourners. I'll be back as soon as possible. I've got to go talk to the parents.'

'What now? They just lost their daughter. We out of all people should...'

I placed my palm upon her chest. 'I have to. They know something. That old lady was not who she said she was and they know it.'

'How the hell do mysteries seem to go out of their way to find you, I do not know?!'

'Some sort of inner mystery magnet, I guess.'

We kissed softly on the lips and walked up the staircase, together. Tracy smiled a smile of support and returned to our room. As she turned on the TV set, ready to be informed on which zodiac sign is better in bed, I walked uneasily in the direction of the palace's master bedroom. The long corridor with the fitted, expensive Persian carpet and the works of art hanging from the walls would have been a delight to explore under any other circumstance. After every two paintings came a closed door. The only door opened was the one opposite the master bedroom. Inside, a large, round pink carpet filled the center of the room. The fuschia walls were decorated with faded Barbie wall stickers. Dolls, teddy bears, boxes of puzzlers and other toys filled the room. An indoor swing stood to my left, while on my right was a large purple sofa, cleverly placed next to the bookshelf filled with childhood gems like the Very Hungry Caterpillar, The Little Prince and Charlotte's Web. Cassandra's childhood playroom. Gaby would have loved this room. My daughter had been a major Barbie fan. Then again, which seven year old girl is not? It is funny how the most insignificant trivia can spark a memory. Gaby and I, in her bedroom having a tea party with her dolls. Now, all I have is memories. Memories of when I used to be a father of a living child and not just a keeper of her memory and her unconditional, innocent, child-to-parent love. Gaby would have been eleven this year. I guess she might have outgrown her Barbies by now. Kids grow up too fast now a days.

I finally managed to pull myself out of those old thoughts and turned towards the master bedroom's door. A short, petite lady in a pink dress stood outside the door, playing nervously with her pearl necklace. I remembered seeing her upon our arrival to the house, yet did not know her name. She had said she was the bride's aunt.

Judging by her pointy ears, her full bottom lip and her deep set eyes, I would bet she was related to Cosma.

Upon my approach, she wiped the tears away from the corner of her eyes and shook her shoulders as to gather herself.

'Hello. I am Captain Papacosta. I am here to talk...'

'Of course, of course,' she was quick to say. 'I am Anneta Zampetaki, Cosma's sister. I found myself coming up here to comfort them and just as I reached the door, I realized, I was the one that needed comfort. I can't go in there. I will just stand there like a fool and cry.' I smile sympathetically.

'Maybe, we could have some tea sent up? That always seems to help.'

'Yes, you're right. Especially, in this horrid weather. Oh, the daughters lost in this world,' she murmured, as she limped down the hallway.

If you only knew...

Irene Zampetaki's sobbing echoed in the hallway, every now and then interrupted by her husband's cry. 'Why, God, why?' he repeated. The knocking on the door brought silence to the room. Neither of them spoke. I built up the courage, knocked again and opened the door slowly.

Cosma sat with his head in trembling hands, rocking back and forth at the edge of his king-sized bed. Irene sat curled up on an oversized armchair with a tall back. The color of her skin reminded me of Tracy's in the days after Gaby's death. She lingered through our apartment, ashen, pale as new paper, as if something unnatural guzzled all life out of her. Her skin was engulfed by sorrow. As if the blood knew to stop flowing as before; the soul with all its pain taking over, leaving an empty vessel of a childless mother behind.

Cosma looked up and squinted his eyes in my direction. Pain and grief furrowed his brow. The look on his face revealed his mind's process to recognize me. 'Ah, yes. The police captain. Costa, right?'

'Yes, sir. Believe me, I am sorry to bother you at such a time. Trust me, I know what you are going through...'

'How could you possibly...' Irene began forming the cliché question.

'My daughter was gunned down in front of my eyes and left her last breath in my arms,' I replied coldly, and continued 'when a murder occurs it is wise to act at once.'

To receive testaments before people have time to come up with a lame story.

'That old lady was not who she said she was, right?'

Both nodded in agreement.

'She wrote she was Maria Marousaki. Wife of Ioanni Marousaki. You know that name, don't you?'

More nodding.

'So, who wants to tell me the story that led to your daughter's death?' I did not mean to sound so cold and distant. I hate it when something sounds right in your head and the moment you utter the words in formation, you realize you could have said it better.

'I realize, Mr Costa, that you were born and raised in America,' Irene said.

'That is correct.'

'I don't know how much you know about Crete and its vendettas.'

Maybe Ioli should have come up and I should have interviewed the guests.

'I know that families can hold grudges that last for decades...'

'Centuries,' Cosma interrupted.

Irene gradually stood up and slowly walked over to the window. The cold winds were throwing droplets of rain against the glass surface, water running down like tears. Irene wiped hers away and eventually spoke in a slow, crackling voice.

'It all started over a hundred years ago, when Cosma's great-grandfather fell in love with Katerina Mamalaki, the daughter of the richest man in Chania at the time. Katerina was to be married off to Christo Marousaki. The Marousaki family were winemakers just like Cosma's family and never really got along...'

Chapter 5

Town Of Chania, Crete 1909

Christo Marousaki, wearing his heavy, black boots, leapt out of the hand-made wooden chair and approached the window. He pushed open the rather dusty persiennes and smiled as the summer breeze swept by him and entered the room.

What a magnificent spring day, what a great day to get married.

He twisted his thick, black mustache with one hand, while with the other he felt his aroused genitals. His sexual fantasies had kept him awake for most of the night. He dreamt over and over again of his wedding night with Katerina. It had been six months since he was first introduced to the sweet, young, beautiful eighteen year old heiress and so far he had only managed to steal a faint kiss on the cheek.

He knelt before his bedside table and kissed his icon of Christ, a gift from his late great-grandmother.

'Thank you, Lord. For...' He paused. He stood tall and proud; a man with many blessings. 'Well, for everything.'

At twenty-three he felt he could climb Psiloriti, Crete's tallest mountain. Handsome, from a prestigious family and as firstborn, heir to the Marousaki winery. And in a few hours, he could add the title of married to Katerina Liontaraki, firstborn of the richest family in Chania.

Miles away, on the other side of Chania, preparations at Liontaraki Manor were in full swing. Servants arranged flowers, laid out freshly cleaned carpets, prepared rooms, polished silverware and dusted –again- spotless surfaces, while below deck, the kitchen cooks prepared the food for the five hundred guests. Barrels of freshly cut vegetables brightened up the cherry wood kitchen while the strong smell of olives filled the air. Ladies bumped into each other as they prepared the village salads and the 'fancy fig and pomegranate salad' that the lady of the house requested. Others peeled and cooked red earth potatoes and the younger ones were in charge of making an array of Cretan desserts. In the next room, men chopped up yesterday's butchered pigs and lambs, and placed the meat on the metal skewers; lemon, salt and virgin olive oil followed on top. Outside, in the spacious back garden tens of tables were laid with fine, white cloths and expensive silverware. In the middle of each table a porcelain vase stood proud, filled with roses cut in the morning.

Meanwhile, in a building tucked out of the way -an abandoned cottage on the grounds of the large estate- Katerina cried in the arms of Theodore Zampetaki.

'You are crazy,' she said and pushed him away.

'Crazy for you, my rose.'

'Don't, please don't call me that.'

'What else would I call the sun of my life, the woman who I love with all my heart, the woman with whom I became one just last night...'

'That was a mistake! I was foolish and acted like a... like a common whore!' Katerina yelled and paced up and down.

Theodore stood opposite her motionless. His heart was ready to burst. 'A whore does not love her clients. You love me, Katerina and there is no denying it!'

'Love can't save us, my dear Theo. My parents have chosen my man, how could we ever...'

'We elope.' He said it as firmly as his trembling lips and weak knees allowed him to. 'Just last year we expelled the Turks. We live in a world where everything is possible.'

'Theo, my parents would...'

A faint smile appeared across his sunburnt face. His green eyes found their sparkle.

'Why are you smiling?'

'You're worried about your parents,' he replied calmly and stepped forward, stopping inches from her face, from her alluring, red lips. 'Which means, my dear, *you* want me. You want to elope with me. You are not thinking of yourself, but of your parents. Well, you know what I say? To hell with them. They are selling you off to create strong ties and ensure your money is invested well.' He grabbed her and kissed her with a passion seen only by people in love, crazy people, young people. And Theo was all three. 'But, they are old and like all that walks this earth, my dear, they are sure to pass on to the next world.' Another kiss. 'We only have a limited time on this planet and I want to spend every second of it with you.' Another kiss. Harder on the lips this time. 'And with our children. Picture them. Our little boy and our beautiful girl.' He rubbed her tummy. Tears fell from Katerina's eyes.

Hours later, many tears were shed at Chania's grand Cathedral. Christo waited and waited, pacing mechanically at the altar. Finally, the message arrived. The bride was nowhere to be found. A note found in her bedroom explaining how she could not go through with the wedding. A second envelope addressed to her mother explained the reasons why.

A genuine Cretan, Christo's first words were a request for his gun. However, his stunning bride and his new arch enemy did not return to Chania until three years had passed and Christo had found and married another lover.

It had been the biggest gossip of 1913. The return of the eloped couple. They had married in a chapel near Rethymno and then lived in a remote village by the sea. Katerina gave birth to twins, a boy and a girl just as promised by Theodoro. Christo still wished to use his rifle; however, his hand was stayed by his pregnant wife. Older, wiser and with a baby on the way, Christo put away his weapon.

Gavdos, 2015

'A truce seemed to be possible, but then again this is Crete,' Irene Zampetaki said with her elegant, cultured voice and paused. She turned her head towards the door.

'Yes?' she replied, to the discreet knocking.

'I brought tea, ma'am,' the shy kitchen maid with the rosy cheeks said. She brought in the silver tray with the blue and white porcelain tea set. She placed it on the wooden, antique coffee table and with a nod she fled the gloom of the room.

Greek hospitality prevailed over any grief and Irene lifted herself out of the armchair and prepared three cups of tea. She did not bother asking me how I take it. She added a spoon of sugar and a few drops of warm milk. The proper way of drinking tea, according to Mrs Zampetaki. She took her cup in her hands and walked over to the oval window. She gazed out towards the horizon. The ocean, like a huge layer of thick oil, unfolded before her eyes. The island was never one of many colors; besides her well maintained garden, the rest was made out of beach sand, dust and thorny bushes of dull green. The only color that ever stood out was the blue of the sky above and its reflection in the cool waters below. Now, the world seemed entirely colorless. Her baby girl was no longer a part of it.

She turned around and looked at me, while taking a sip from her hot beverage. Strands of steam threaded past her empty eyes. Lightning flashed through the window, darkening her figure.

'Shall we get back to our story?'

Chania had grown into one of the finest towns of the Cretan state, now officially part of Greece, again. In the calm waters of the harbor, Venetian buildings were reflected in the moving sea, swirling around, bringing Van Gogh paintings to shame. Proud, muscular horses pulled carriages along the paved road, carrying their masters past the many tavernas that had opened along the coast. Cretans had always enjoyed their meat and their wine.

Two wineries competed to prevail in the booming market. The Zampetaki winery and the Marousaki winery. Both, were family run. The Zampetaki winery by Theodoro and his son Kyriako and the Marousaki winery by Christo Marousaki and his two sons. His wife Maria was pregnant with a third son at the time.

Like with all sad stories, a series of seemingly unconnected events would lead to death. If only Kyriako Zampetaki had woken up a few minutes later that day, or earlier for that matter. If only he enjoyed his morning coffee for longer.

Christo Marousaki stood in the doorway of his 19th century log house, kissing his wife goodbye, before heading out to the vineyards and then to the winery. His large hands caressed her six month baby bump.

'If it's a boy again, I want to call him Ioanni, after my mother Ioanna.'

'That's a lovely thought,' she replied with a smile and leaned her head upon his chest, her honey-colored hair swirling in the wind.

'Bye, mama,' Constantino flew past them first. 'Bye, mama.' Antony followed.

'Wait, you two,' their father's voice brought the youthful enthusiasm to a halt. 'You're not coming with me. I need you to ride into town and pick up the new barrels from Mister Papadopoulos.'

Both grinned at each other. At sixteen and eighteen years of age, they enjoyed nothing more than to ride their horses into town and pose for the fine ladies of the town.

'Behave,' their mother said, widening her brown eyes.

'Don't we always?' Antony said, as he jumped upon his white horse.

Both parents remained in each other's arms as they watched their sons ride off into the morning sun.

Some ideas are born out of nowhere, somewhere deep inside our minds. Kyriako Zampetaki found himself riding to Katrakis barber shop, instead of up to the winery. The Katrakis barber shop was situated on the main road, heading down to the pier, right next to Mister Papadopoulos's workplace.

The two brothers arrived upon their well-groomed, agile horses just as Kyriako hopped off his tied-up steed and said hello to Mister Papadopoulos.

'Since when do they let riff-raff come to this end of town?' Antony mocked him.

Kyriako ignored the insult. He bowed his head and tilted his hat to Mister Papadopoulo, turned his back to the two brothers and walked steadily towards the barber shop's open door.

'Cutting his hair to become more presentable? Maybe he wishes to find another rich whore to support their pitiful winery,' Constantino said, while a grin was born across his round face.

Kyriako froze on the spot. He turned his head slightly around and without looking at them asked 'Are you referring to my mother, sir?'

Both brothers laughed. 'Yes, *sir*! What are you going to do about it?

'You'll soon find out,' Kyriako replied and entered the barber shop. He exhaled deeply and complimented himself for keeping his cool. No punishment for calling his mother a whore could be executed before public eyes.

Two days later, the unfortunate news spread from mouth to mouth in the small community. Fire had burned down the Marousaki winery, destroying the entire wooden building and killing its owner, Christo Marousaki and his two sons along the way. All three burnt alive, trapped inside their beloved winery.

Maria went into premature labor upon hearing the news of the loss of her entire family. Her precious boys and the love of her life, gone, dead. All will to live floated away from her, leaving behind an empty vessel. A human without a soul.

Doctors did not expect the six and half month old baby to survive the long night, but the Greek sun sneaked out of the endless ocean and bright light lit up the dark hospital room to reveal a very much alive infant. Maria forced herself out of the rusty, old bed with the once white linen and staggered towards her baby boy. Her eyes came back to life, shining brighter than summer's midday sun.

'My little warrior... Ioanni,' she said and ran her index finger on her baby's red cheek. Little Ioanni opened his eyes and Maria would swear that she saw him smiling. Ioanni survived all the nights that followed and months later, Maria returned to her empty home with a healthy boy in her arms. A boy that would grow up listening to stories how the Zampetaki family murdered his father and brothers. A boy that turned into a weakling by Cretan standards. A man that never acted upon his family's vendetta due to walking problems, a weak heart and a weaker spirit. A man who on his death bed asked his elderly soon-to-be widow and his tall, muscular, mean-spirited sons to offer him the revenge he never took himself.

Chapter 6

Tragedies in Greece are dealt with in numbers. Whether you lost a loved one, were involved in a car accident, got diagnosed with an incurable disease or got fired, it was expected that nearly everyone in your life would gather around you.

Ioli paused outside the dining room door, closed her eyes, calmed her nerves and brought distance between herself and the case. With steady footsteps, she entered the lavish room.

Homer sat frozen in a high back, opulent designer armchair. Cretans did not cry, at least not in public, and there must have been a dozen people around him. His brother, Jason stood behind him with his hand on his brother's shoulder. His face and pose betraying how uncomfortable and helpless he felt. Mark leaned on the wall behind them, forcing a short-lived smile as Ioli walked towards them. The room was silent. Even Homer's mother cried in silence, held close by her husband.

Homer did not move a muscle. His broad shoulders were still as mountains; his legs firmly sunk into the Persian carpet. Ioli approached, knelt before him and gazed into his trembling, watery eyes. She placed her head upon his chest and hugged him. His heart palpitated, echoing in her ear.

So much for maintaining distance, she thought.

'We need to talk, alone.'

Homer took his time to raise his head. Drained of inner strength, he resisted declining. Better Ioli than any stranger cop from the mainland.

'Let's not ask them all to leave,' he breathily whispered -as much as a Cretan man could whisper. 'It is their loss, too. Come, follow me to my father-in-law's office... *Father-in-law*, hmm,' he said mocking the word. 'It is true, then, that the whole thing seems so unreal, so distant,' he said, standing up.

The two walked slowly out of the room, down the long corridor with the expensive art, by paintings that you had to read the caption underneath to understand what they depicted.

'I think we could all use a good drink,' Kallisto spoke first, breaking the silence of the room. 'What?' she asked, with eyes wide open, when her boyfriend Leonida shot a disapproving -and in her opinion judgemental- look her way. 'They're all just standing around staring at Homer. Look at them. As if they haven't seen death or sorrow before. They need a drink.'

'She's right,' cousin George said, listening in on their conversation. 'Excuse me?' he nodded over to the maid, standing awkwardly by the doorway. 'Could we have some drinks served?'

'What do you have in mind, sir?'

'Anything alcoholic,' Kallisto replied. 'Whiskey for us, wine for the old ladies, ouzo for the men and probably some weak vodka oranges for her friends,' she ordered, looking over the maid's shoulder at Cassandra's friends. Alexandra, Andrea, Jenny and Amanda held hands and occasionally hugged whatever member of the group next succumbed to tears.

Jason, also, looked upon the group, fighting against an inner desire to walk over and comfort Amanda.

'Go on over,' Mark urged him.

Jason swung round. 'Too obvious?'

'To me at least.'

'A dame in distress, in a castle's dining room with the fireplace lit and a storm menacing outside. Under other circumstances, this would be one soppy romance tale. But, no. It would be in bad taste,' Jason said, took the first drink from the tray that floated before his eyes, held professionally by the maid who entered the room, and walked off. 'I'm going up.'

Homer slid the office's glass doors to their respective sides. A deep breath of shock came from the corner of the room. Homer's hand searched for the light; the thick curtains preventing any light from entering the octagon shaped room from outside. Homer lowered the switch and the fluorescent lights flickered to life, revealing Melissa sitting on the lilac sofa with the golden plated frame.

She immediately stood up and as always when faced with people, she lowered and tilted her head to an angle that hid her horrific markings. Or so, she wished to believe.

'I'm sorry,' she quickly uttered, and rushed to leave the room. 'I'm so sorry for your loss,' she said with the same speed, as she walked past Homer, who dragged himself through the room and fell into the soft sofa.

'What were you doing here?' Ioli asked, stepping in front of Melissa as she exited the room.

'Oh, I...' she started to say, looked into the room and lowered her voice to such a level that even Ioli struggled to hear.

'Death brings no sadness to me. Call it apathy. Call me insensitive, but I lost my parents, my sister and half my face in that fire and I know how fragile and cruel life can be. I cannot stand in a room watching people cry, when my eyes are incapable of tears or any emotions of sorrow.'

Ioli forced a flat smile. 'I understand,' she said and with that Melissa was off. Ioli exhaled, crunched her knuckles and entered the room with the thought that in this life, you never know what you are going to hear.

Or see.

As Ioli entered the room, loud thuds echoed through the house. The deluge raged outside and strong winds knocked over the array of flowerpots that were once the pride and joy of Mr Zampetaki. Suddenly, a large branch from the lemon tree that stood proudly just outside the office broke off and slammed through the office window. Pieces of glass shot and scattered through the room. Ioli managed to duck in time, her reflexes always a strong point, however, Homer received multiple scratches on his arms and a couple on his face. Crimson lines shortly appeared on his forehead and cheeks.

'Not my day, huh, universe?' he asked, looking out the smashed window. 'Quick, let's go to the next room, before everyone comes and makes a fuss,' Homer said, passing by Ioli who stood, admiring his attitude. Homer opened the next door without knocking. The mansion's laundry room light was on, though no machinery was at work. Katerina, the tall maid, sat on a wooden bench, her eyes swollen from her on-going tears. The smoke from her slim cigarette circled her head before travelling to the barely opened window.

'I'm sorry...' both said simultaneously.

Katerina bowed her head, threw her lit cigarette out to be eaten by the storm and faltered by Homer.

'Are you okay?' Homer asked, placing his hand on Katerina's shoulder. Katerina's eyes moved around rapidly, without staring at anything in specific. A third generation maid, taught well to never make direct eye contact or start conversations with any members of the family. Some traditions so outdated, yet so hard to change, especially in the countryside. Especially now, when most maids, cleaners and gardeners were immigrants from countries worse off; immigrants who had no idea of their rights.

'Oh, yes, sir. Though, I am the one that should be asking you? My sincere condolences.'

'Thank you.' Homer forced another smile; another pointless, meaningless smile. Condolences are just a word, just something people around the grieving one need to say. People need to act, have an inner need to help, but, in tragic situations like these, nothing can be done. Homer's Cassandra would never be coming back, so we say a word and move on.

Homer sat down on the bench, his eyes examining his cuts.

'Katerina? You were the one who found the body, right?' Ioli asked, bringing Katerina to a halt. Katerina placed her right hand, upon her chest that moved up and down from her heavy breathing. She swallowed hard, and then opened her mouth, but the words never came out. A single forty year old and a resident of an island of fifty, this was the first body she had seen. The covered with blood room and the sliced open throat of the bride, did not help the experience. Katerina finally nodded, realizing she had not answered Ioli's question.

'I understand how stressful it must have been for you, but I need you to think hard and remember, was the door locked?'

Katerina's eyes looked up and then journeyed down and met Ioli's. 'Closed, but not locked.'

'Was there any blood on the handle?'

'No, no blood. Though, it was raining hard.'

'Have you been to the pool house before?'

'Yes, many times.'

'Notice anything out of place? Anything peculiar?'

'No... Well, after seeing Miss Cassandra, I just fled the room, screaming.'

'Thank you, Katerina. If you remember anything, anything at all, just let me know.'

Katerina nodded, bowed her head and without saying another word, left the low ceilinged room. Katerina's perfume lingered in the stale, confined air. Ioli enjoyed a whiff of the lemony scent and sat down beside Homer. His hands were icy cold, his eyes colder.

'If you are not ready...'

'Come on, cuz. Don't go soft because it's me. Do your cop routine and I'll be fine. I'm a big boy now; you don't have to protect me anymore.'

Ioli leaned her head upon his trembling shoulder. 'If only it was as simple as beating up the bully that took your lunch money.'

'As simple? You beat up guys twice our size, and with ease I may add. Simple!' Homer chuckled. 'Fuck memory lane,' he suddenly said. 'Tell me what really happened. What did that old bitch do to Cassandra?'

Anger. Always there. Alongside the confusion, the sorrow, the regrets, the pain, anger always gave a show.

'Homer...'

'Don't *Homer* me like that! Give me the details.'

'She was stabbed. She died within minutes. There is nothing else I can tell you at the moment. What's important, now, is for you to remember anything Cassandra may have said about any quarrels, any misunderstandings, any...'

Homer shook his head the entire time. 'She was lovable,' was all he whispered.

'When did you last see her?'

'Last night. We stood in my bedroom's doorway, joking how this would be our first and last night apart. I should never have left her...'

'What time was this?'

'Must have been around half past twelve. After midnight for sure.'

'Why would she be out at the pool house? And in her wedding dress, too?'

'That is where she kept it. She did not want to risk me seeing it. She was quite the superstitious type.' Homer's eyes shined a shade brighter. 'Well, I be damned. That old witch had sat with Cassandra just before dinner and spoke about her wedding day and how the night before she just had to try on her wedding dress, one more time. She said she slept in it. It was a funny story, actually. Guess the joke is on me.'

'Oh, my God.' Voices were heard from the office next door.

'Guess they found the tree,' Homer said, stood up and mechanically walked out the room. Mark stood in the long corridor.

'What the hell? You're cut.' His doctoring instincts kicked in; he placed his arm around Homer, who in a zombie-like state followed his friend into the kitchen.

I traipsed past the on-going commotion in the office, with Herculean Cretans -led by Uncle Thomas- trying to push the thick tree back out of the window while their wives gave them instructions. Freezing air attacked through the window, carrying icy droplets and dried up leaves from the ground below, and that ground was disappearing, sinking, turning into a watery world. Mark had informed me of Ioli's whereabouts. I found her alone, lost in thought. She heard my heavy footsteps and raised her honey-colored eyes in my direction.

'Finished with the parents?'

I nodded and sat down beside her, stretching my long, tired legs. Now, my knees were aching greatly. My body, once my temple, was now an old car begging for new parts. 'Got a long vendetta story out of the mother. Seems like a classic revenge story.'

'I hate clichés, but I'm too drained to think. I'm all ears.'

Ioli sat quietly and listen to my re-telling of the story that began over one hundred years ago. She did not speak until I had reached the end of the horrible tale.

'And she waited until the poor girl's fucking wedding day to take revenge on her husband's behalf?'

'Hate can be the most powerful emotion.'

'Well, I hate all this shit going on. And I'm telling you, I'm sure the old lady had help.'

'Maybe someone wrote her letter before she came. From what Mr Zampetaki told me, she had kids. Two sons. I called Headquarters and have asked for a check up on her. I want to know if she travelled alone. How did she show up here, pretending to be aunt Myrrine and no one questioned anything?'

'Well, to my family's defense, no one had seen aunt Myrrine since she left for America fifty or so years ago. I called HQ, too. I asked for background checks on all the guests I do not know personally. I need no more shocks. Like one of the bridesmaids turning out to be her daughter or some crazy shit like that.'

'You curse more when you're worked up.'

'Doesn't everybody?'

'Guess so. How's Homer?'

'Acting strong and keeping silent. Greek male DNA. He last saw her when they separated last night. Seems like he did not have a clue that she would go down to the pool house. She said she was going to bed. I think we have to talk to her friends, they might know more.'

Knocking on the door echoed through the badly lit laundry room. Mark stood by the door with an awkward smile below his kind hazelnut eyes.

'Sorry for interrupting. Homer wants to go see the body.'

'In this weather?' I asked.

Mark raised his hands. 'I think it will help it set in. The initial shock is still with him.'

Ioli stood up with that determined look that suited her so well. She wore confidence over all other emotions. 'Just the four of us, though.'

Like most crazy decisions in life, things took place in minutes. Our warm bodies welcomed our dried coats and out into the continual downpour we went. The ceaseless rain gathered into large puddles that covered the distance between the mansion and the pool house. My hand fiddled around in my turned-dark-brown-by-the-rain trouser's left pocket and with the key in hand, I led the party of four, through a rain Noah and his ark would be proud of, to the safety of the inner environment. An environment now of blood and of the body of a girl whose life was cut short just at the worst time imaginable.

Homer fell to his knees and with Ioli's hands upon his shoulders, he finally let the tears fall. His right hand caressed Cassandra's bare leg. He did not dare approach her face. Her bruised from the fall face, her bloody back and her cut open throat were too much for him to bear.

'Goodbye, baby.' He placed two fingers upon his dry, pale lips, kissed them and carried the kiss to her icy skin.

A painful sight to witness, though my attention was drawn to the stabbing wound of the neck. I have seen my fair share of stabbings in my line of duty and have observed many messy wounds. This one was so precise, so surgical. Never mind the steady handwriting; the old lady had one hell of a steady hand indeed.

If she stabbed the girl, that is...

Chapter 7

Mrs Irene Zampetaki stood naked in the middle of her private, en suite, deluxe bathroom. A smile of sorrow was etched across her aging face. As peculiar as it may sound, this was her favorite place to be; the room she took the longest to design and decorate. The round tub in the center of the room, the colossal mirror with the golden frame overlooking the pure African granite basins, the expensive marble tiles, even the various oil based candles; all chosen carefully from an array of choices. Fresh flowers were brought up daily every morning, while a tall glass of chardonnay arrived every evening to accompany Irene on her mission of resisting modern, hectic life. That is how she viewed showers; part of a new lifestyle, a lifestyle she wished not to belong to. She wanted to soak in the bath tub for an hour, enjoying Maria Callas, Vivaldi and Bach; all her favorites. How insignificant it all seemed to her now. She knew she had to force herself to wash and get ready for dinner. Dead daughter or not, Greek hospitality was alive and she had dozens of guests gathered in the dining room below. She stood in front of the mirror, unconsciously checking her body like she did every time before a bath and found herself focusing on her tummy. Her hands rubbed her belly and tears streaked down her ashen face. She had once carried Cassandra inside her. Flashbacks of memories catalysed her mind. Her baby girl that she would have died to protect was no longer a part of the world of the living. Irene fought for air. The room, now cold and hostile, was suffocating her. She rushed to the window and pulled down the handle, pushing the tinted glass window open. Cold, freezing air jetted inside and dried her running tears. Just then, loud thunder roared mightily.

Thunder that shook the very ground.

'My God, what shitty weather,' Uncle Thomas said downstairs, and gulped down his ice-free scotch.

'Shh, Thomas,' his wife, Georgia, protested and drank the last drops of her red wine.

Everyone stood around, talking in a whispery manner and drinking their favorite alcoholic beverage.

Ioli sat between her parents on the violet sofa opposite the grand fireplace with the tall candlesticks and the never used candles.

'Is there not a priest in the nearby village to come and bless the body? It's unholy to leave the body locked up in the pool house. She should be brought in, put in her bed,' Anna spoke with eyes wide open and hands clumsily stroking one another.

'What village?' Gianni replied. 'The ten flies that live on this God-forsaken rock of an island? There's no priest, right Ioli? Ioli?'

'I don't think she is listening to us,' Anna leaned forward and said to her husband.

Ioli was listening; she was not paying attention, though. Her eyes and mind were scanning the room, examining every guest. Their posture, the way they talked, who they talked to, what they said. She was convinced the old lady had help.

Cassandra's four bridesmaids stood together, holding hands, comforting each other by the enormous oval window and in silence stared at the falling rain, streaking down the glass. Too young and too much in shock to speak, they drifted through the foreign environment together, wishing for the storm to cease. They had decided to stay to bury their friend and then catch the first flight out to America.

'We stood by her in life and we will stand by her in death,' Amanda had put it.

'There she goes again with her corny day time TV lines,' Alexandra whispered to Jenny.

Katerina, the maid, passed by with Kallisto's cosmopolitan in hand. She looked distraught, probably because Kallisto had returned the previous beverage with the complaint of it not being strong enough.

'Too virgin for my liking, dear,' she had said and it had taken Katerina a few seconds before realizing what the star had meant.

'No drink for you?' Kallisto asked frail Melissa, who sat in a dark corner behind the mahogany bar. Melissa did not reply, much to Kallisto's annoyance. She did not intend on acting nice and struggled to fight her repulsion upon looking at Melissa's disfigured face. 'I asked if...' she raised her voice.

'I heard you the first time. No need to act nice. I do not intend on acting social either. Don't stress your pretty little face over me. I'm fine, thank you very much, I have ordered coffee.'

Kallisto never backed out of a fight. She thrived for drama and had a stinger of a tongue.

'If I was George, I would poison your coffee, you miserable witch.'

'If I was Leonida, I'd drink it!' Melissa replied and discreetly got up, leaving the room with Churchill on her mind.

Their boyfriends, George and Leonida, stood by the dining table, unaware of their other half's petty quarrel.

'I can't believe it. Poor Homer. Imagine losing your person like that,' Leonida said.

'Shit happens,' George replied and placed his hands upon Leonida's arms.

'That's very philosophical of you,' Leonida replied in obvious non-joking state. 'And we look like fools. We should have brought black.'

'How were we supposed to know we would need black clothes? By the way, I think you look great in your blue suit.'

'Just get me another drink,' Leonida said, handing him his empty wine glass, for the third time.

At that moment, Jason and Mark entered the room. Both looking smart with their formal evening wear on. Jason had shaved and a goatee hung from his strong jaw. A goatee that served as an ice-breaker, when Amanda and Andrea approached him. The other two girls had left the room. Ioli never understood the logic in group visits to the bathroom.

As Tracy and I arrived for dinner, Mark had finally picked up the courage to approach Ioli in front of her parents. A mindless comment about the weather was all he managed to utter.

'Ladies and gentlemen, if you please, take your seats. Dinner is ready,' the chubby chef announced in a deep voice.

'But are we going to eat without our hosts?' Anna wondered, just as Ioli was introducing Mark, explaining who he was. That thought was on most minds as guests in and out of the room gathered to be seated. Minutes later, the first freshly cut salads decorated with homemade feta and olive oil arrived. Greek bread followed with olives and dozens of little, white porcelain plates filled with various dips.

Just then a chilling scream reverberated through the house, journeying from the floor above and entering the dining room, chilling us to the bone. A second scream by the same female voice followed, bringing us to our feet. Ioli and I led the group that rushed up the red carpet stairs and towards the directions of the scream. By the time we reached the top, Mr Zampetaki's voice boomed loud and clear.

'No, no. God, no. Please, no. Baby. Baby, talk to me!'

Outside the bathroom door, sat Christina, the maid that had fainted upon delivering the news of Cassandra's death. Katerina rushed to her and knelt down before her, her long arms embracing the shaking young girl.

'Madame has killed herself,' she managed to say as I approached the bathroom door.

'Stay here,' Ioli ordered the rest of the guests and followed me. No one entered the bedroom.

The floor was slippery with water from the bathtub. Cosma Zampetaki was leaning in the tub, holding his wife tight; shaking her and begging her to wake up. Bottles of prescription medicine floated in the tub beside Irene's naked, pale body. I stepped carefully towards them, my fingers searching for a pulse both on her neck and wrist. She was dead. I shook my head towards Ioli, who had found a nylon bag in which to place the emptied bottles.

Cosma's eyes eagerly waited for me to speak. The silence was deafening. I swallowed hard, clearing my throat as if it would make my next words come out and sound better.

'I'm sorry, Cosma, she is...'

'No, no. Say it isn't so.' He turned towards his wife's hollow eyes. 'Why, baby, why?'

To lose your daughter and wife in the same day. The two women in his life, gone, vanished, slipped away.

'I should just end my life right now and turn this house into a mausoleum,' Cosma said, jumping into the tub with his wife, forcing his head under water.

'Ioli, help me,' I cried out, trying to pull the heavy man out of the water. Mark entered the room at that moment, having patiently waited outside, just in case Irene was still alive and in need of medical attention. The three of us pulled the man out of the tub.

'Come with me,' Ioli said to the grieving man and led him by the hand outside to the hallway, for him to be with his relatives. His sister, Anneta, struggled to rush to and embrace her brother. Within each other's arms, they knelt on the floor, their tears falling free from their red, sore eyes.

Inside the bathroom, Mark swayed slightly as he approached the floating body.

'You okay?' I queried.

Mark lifted his hand. 'I'm fine. Just shook up from all... this. You know, I practiced as a surgeon, but I ended up in pediatrics. Could not take all the seriously injured turning into bodies,' he said, coming closer. 'I'm opening my own practice soon,' he added, his eyes searching for a reaction from Ioli.

He checked for vital signs and then, examined the body.

'Though the water is cold, she is still quite warm. For a body, that is. She probably dozed off and drowned in the last twenty minutes or so.'

I fiddled around in my deep trouser pockets in search for my new phone. I had never been a fan of modern technology or had ever wished to be up to date with all the scientific leaps that were being taken in the field of cell phones; however, this was one of those rare occasions where I was glad my previous grandpa phone had broken. It fell to its final resting ground, one warm winter day, when against every logic Tracy took me rock-climbing. Now, not only did I own a shiny, touch screen, multi-functional, smarter-than-your-average-Joe phone (according to the over-excited sales boy), I had finally learnt how to use the basics. And taking photographs was one of my newly obtained skills.

I switched on the red angle poise floor lamp and directed its light towards Irene's face. I carefully pushed back her wet hair and held her face towards my phone. The clicking of the phone breaking the deadly silence of the room as Mark stood to the side and observed me.

'Notice anything, boss?' Ioli inquired, reentering the room. I did not answer immediately, yet she did not mind. She seemed preoccupied with sniffing the air and falling into deep thought.

'What are you doing?' I could not resist asking.

'Lemons,' she enigmatically answered. 'You?'

'Look around her mouth.'

Ioli squatted down, her feline eyes focusing, sending messages to her analytical brain.

'My, my. The plot thickens.'

'What's going on?' Mark finally asked.

'Mark, I am going to have to ask you to leave the room. This is off limits, too. Just like the pool house. Let everyone know, that no one is allowed in here,' I firmly said. Without any sort of remark, Mark walked out the room, his worried eyes focused on Ioli.

Chapter 8

City Of Athens, years ago

Agatha sighed in relief as the plane's front wheel – or was it the back ones that made contact first? - touched the sizzling runway of Ellinikon Athens Airport. Her very first journey on a plane had come to an end. She carefully watched and followed the other passengers through all the necessary procedures out of fear of getting lost. It was her second visit to Athens, the first being with her parents and younger sister, having travelled from Chania by ship. It had been July and a cruise ship was family voted as the top choice for a summer vacation. They sailed to the paradises of Mykonos and Santorini before heading to the port of the big city, when in autumn she would start her new life as an architecture student.

Now, the calendar read September the 4th and she exited the glass doors of the busy airport alone. The Greek sun, a fireball in the sky, was aggressive on her light-colored skin. The wind, thick and stuffy, made it hard to breathe. Nothing compared to the sea breeze and fresh island air she was used to.

Eighteen year old Agatha wrapped her silky, blond hair in a high bun, stroked her flowery, knee length dress that had more wrinkles than her grandmother and wheeled her pink suitcase to the taxi cabs that seemed to be melting under the sun opposite the road. Her blue eyes sparkled with joy as she thought how lucky she was to be able to afford a taxi. The sight of the overcrowded, blue city bus sent shivers down her spine.

Feeling the male eyes of the drivers upon her, Agatha's pale skin turned rosy around her high cheekbones. She headed for the first taxi in the lane and wished the overweight driver with the military boots a good day.

The bald driver turned around and flashed a row of yellowy teeth.

'Well, good day to you too, little Miss. Welcome to Athens,' he said and rushed to load her luggage into the back of the car. He slammed down the green taxi's trunk, scratched his chest hair that was overflowing out of his open to the belly button, checked shirt and at his top speed –which is not saying much- opened the back door for her. Agatha smiled politely and entered the vehicle, careful the twirling wind did not lift up her dress. The whole car shook as Mr Petride A.K.A. typical Greek cab driver jumped into the front seat.

'Where to, little lady?'

'Apostolou Pavlou 8, Thiseio, please,' Agatha replied with her cultured, gentle voice.

'Fancy neighborhood for a student,' Mr Petride commented, as the car's engine roared to life.

'My mother insisted on a view of the Acropolis and near the tourist area. They plan to come often for holidays.' Mr Petride just nodded his head and lit his thick-smoke-producing cheap cigar.

'It will be cheaper than a hotel,' Agatha rushed to add, remembering her father's advice to not show *too rich* and his long list of what to-do and what not-to-do in the big city. Fathers will be fathers, especially when it involves their little girl.

'Sure, sure,' the driver grunted and turned on the radio.

'I love Sfakianaki's new record, don't you?'

'Of course,' she lied.

Her newly-built, brand new two bedroom apartment awaited her on the fourth floor. Agatha eagerly unlocked the front door and rushed into apartment 401. A whiff of strawberries welcomed her in. She looked around, admiring all the perfectly set furniture. The glass coffee table with the strawberry-scented leaves placed in a Swarovski bowl, the expensive TV set, the orange couch that unfolded into a bed, the abstract art on the magnolia painted walls and the green bean bags placed a wide smile under her tiny-for-a-Greek nose. Mother's designer had set everything in place just the week before.

The ecstatic youth yelled a prolonged *oh, yeah,* and proceeded to dance a jig across the zebra-patterned carpet. Agatha, then, kicked off her pink high heels that had cut their way into her flesh and ran into the bedroom, hopping on the king size bed.

'My very own place!' she said out loud as if to validate the situation, to prove this was really happening. She got up and pulled back the heavy curtains. Her hand lifted up the balcony door lock and out she went into the hot, heavy, smoky air of Athens. She leaned on the metal rail, her sight travelling from the traffic jam below, along the multiple coffee shops of the prestigious area of Thiseio, to the most beautiful walk path in the world, named Plaka, all the way up to the grand temple of the Parthenon -Athena's worship ground, placed in the center of the Acropolis.

'So, this is what on top of the world feels like,' she whispered.

'So, this is my new shitty dump,' Achilles said, walking into his below ground, dark, studio apartment in a run-down area of Athens. He, too, had just entered his new apartment.

'What did you expect, my king? Buckingham palace for your ass as you study?' his father mocked him. 'We are very lucky your cousins found this place for you at such a good price.'

Achilles pushed back his hair dangling in front of his eyes, and looked at the feet of passersby on the bustling pavement above. 'Lucky, indeed.'

'Boy, save your irony for school. Don't let any of those fancy professors put you down.'

'Put me down? Isn't everyone in the big city jealous of farm boys like me?'

'There's the spirit! Now, unpack your things while I have a shower. We are meeting up with your cousins tonight for a tour of Athens. I can't wait to hit the night clubs.'

'Now I know why mama said to keep an eye on you. Sometimes, I truly do wonder who the grown-up here is.'

'Don't worry, son. I'll behave, and if any women hit on me, I'll surely send them your way,' his father said and with heavy laughter stripped down to his underwear and headed to the shower.

'Sunday you're leaving, right?' Achilles asked, shaking his head. His father did love embarrassing him, but he was his best friend and the most remarkable man he had ever met. And with that thought, Achilles started to unpack his few humble belongings.

Fate, here in Greece, is a real person; for many just as real as you and me. *Moira* the modern Greeks call her, while the ancients believed there were three of them, the Moires. Fate plays an important role in everyday life, though mostly as an excuse for bad situations. 'It was his fate,' someone would say at every funeral and upon hearing any sort of bad news.

However, every now and then, she is called upon in situations of unparalleled love, and what stronger love than teenage love between two eighteen year olds. Fate is enamored with her classic stories, and two months after their arrival in Athens, on a cold, November morning, a rich girl from Chania and a farmer boy from Crete's countryside boarded the same morning bus.

Chapter 9

Thunder shook the bathroom's thin window glass, reminding us of the mayhem going on outside. We were stranded on a remote island with no police force and two dead bodies. Three, counting the old lady who wheeled herself off the cliff; unless she was somewhere in hiding. Though I had a hard time picturing the near centenarian lady wobbling off into the storm, in the middle of the night, down to the village.

'Irene was murdered?' Ioli asked, closing the beige wooden door behind Mark.

'Sure looks like it. Look, here,' I said, pointing to Irene's cheeks. Two faint red marks graced her pale skin.

'Someone held her mouth open,' Ioli said, examining the body closer.

'... Pushed down the pills and waited for her to sleep...'

'And then just let her slide into the water and drown,' Ioli continued my sentence.

We both stood up and took a second. Ioli stretched her arms up high and tiptoed around the tub, slowly breathing in and out. I just closed my eyes. Each to his own method of concentrating.

Ioli spoke first. 'OK, so obviously someone did not count on police being here and thought to make this look like a suicide. That someone was most likely the old lady's assistant in murdering the bride. I believe the old lady's suicide was to make everyone think there was no other murderer and have them write this off as a suicide,' she said, pointing at Irene. 'And all this to revenge Cosma? Why not kill him or his sister?' she continued with her flow of thought.

'Killing him gives no satisfaction to whoever is behind this. Watching him suffer is enticing, thrilling to the murderer.' I looked straight at Ioli. 'I was upstairs with Tracy at the time; half an hour ago. You were down stairs. Who was missing?'

Ioli pulled up her silky black hair and rolled it up in a bun. She took a hair clip out of her navy blue purse with the pink outline and placed in it her curled up hair.

'I was with my parents and my uncle Thomas with auntie Georgia were behind us the whole time. Leonida and George were there together when I arrived and never left the room. Kallisto arrived minutes later and also did not leave the room. These are really the only ones I can be sure of never leaving the room. Melissa was there from the beginning, but left at one point after bitchiness between her and Kallisto occurred. However, I'm pretty sure she did not go up the stairwell, she turned left and headed down the hall. Maybe, a trip to the toilet? She was back within ten minutes tops.'

'We'll have to ask.'

'Katerina the maid kept coming and going. Though, she would have enough time, if she wished to.'

'What's that look in your eye?'

'I smelled her perfume in here when I entered before. It was the same lemony fragrance she wore downstairs. Talking about the personnel, Christina was up here...'

'The girl that keeps fainting?'

'Could be an act?'

'Oscar-worthy for sure. Cosma was up here, too.'

'And killed his wife?'

'Oldest story in the book.'

Ioli raised her eyebrows and continued. 'We should check that all personnel were in the kitchen at the time. Now, for the ones that easily had the time and we'll have to check them for alibis.'

'Shoot.'

'Homer was a no show, yet do you blame him?'

'If he knew about the vendetta he could have wished for revenge...'

'With all of us around? Hours after losing his wife? Anyway, his parents weren't down for dinner either, so there is a good chance they were all together.'

She spoke faster than usual. The idea of a family member being a murderer did not sit well with her code of honor. She would arrest her own mother if she was guilty. 'Who else?' I asked, pulling her away from those thoughts.

'Two of her bridesmaids left the room together, went up the stairs and never came back down. Alexandra and the other red-headed one. Cosma's sister never came down either. She could have been with her mother. I haven't seen the old lady since breakfast. Jason and Mark came down late...'

'Dreamy Mark could be a suspect for you?'

'Grow up, boss,' she said with a strict tone of her voice, though the corners of her lips gave her away.

'That's quite a list of suspects.'

'Well, let's do what we do best. Let's get investigating.'

'And how are we going to go about it? Don't forget *they*...' I raised my palm and showed towards the direction of the door '... think that the old lady killed Cassandra and Irene committed suicide. She already tried to throw herself off the cliff.'

Ioli took her usual ten seconds to come up with a plan. 'We will announce that we will need everybody's statements about their whereabouts. Typical police procedure for needed paperwork, we will call it. Just to have everything ready for when the weather clears up. That way everyone will get to leave immediately and go home. They will love that part. They are dying to get off this island... sorry, poor choice of words. This way we will also get everybody's whereabouts during the first murder and try through conversation to find out any gossip or information about others.'

'OK, go tell...'

'No, it's got to be you. I'm family. Besides, you're the man-captain in charge and these are Cretans. They're not used to listening to a woman.' She could not help but smile. She unloosened her hair and straightened her knee-high, black dress.

'You look lovely by the way.'

'Thanks boss. I was saving this for a special occasion. I feel a bit of a fool, investigating murders with a dress and make-up.'

'Who knew, right? Anyway, grandma always said it wasn't the vestment that made the priest.'

Ioli chuckled and I asked what was on her mind. 'Don't you ever feel like murders seem to find us? We came for a festive vacation to get away from it all and here we are in the middle of fucking nowhere and bodies piling up around us.'

'You have to admit our lives are never dull. Anyway, I'm old. I'll soon retire and live out my golden years being as dull as paint.'

'You're fifty. You're not old.'

'Then why do I need help getting up from the floor?' I asked with my hand extended, reaching out to her. My legs had gone numb, kneeling for so long on the hard, cold tiled surface. My back ached again, sending those annoying mini vibrations through me.

Oh, yes. I'm not old at all!

People comforting each other filled the long corridor. Their whispering voices and gentle sobbing was covered by the sound of the still-plummeting rain. The constant loud bangs of thunder were starting to annoy me. The lack of sleep and dinner combined with the weather created a super migraine in my frontal lobe. I remembered how aggravated Ioli got when hungry.

'Maybe we should let them eat first? Dinner is served downstairs.'

'You think they would?'

I shrugged my shoulders. Every person standing in the hallway turned to stare at us. I coughed to clear my throat and announced Ioli's plan.

'What? Now?' Anneta objected to the plan first. 'My brother is in no state to...'

I held out my palm and with a calm smile signalled her to stop. 'I understand your brother's state better than anyone. We will speak to him when he is ready. We are all going to go down and eat and then, one by one you will come and give a statement to us in the library.'

'What's really going on, Captain?' Jason's booming voice came from the back of the group.

'Nothing, just procedure.' My voice trained to lie effectively.

'Bullshit, I think...'

'Jason!' his brother's voice cut him off. 'We have had enough drama. For once in your life, just do as you're told,' a teary-eyed Homer said, appearing with his parents by his side. Homer fell to the ground next to his would-have-been father-in-law, his large right arm embracing him.

'My dear, dear boy. We have both lost our loved ones.' Cosma's words came out with difficulty, choked by tears and heavy breathing.

Thunder reminded us of the world outside and our isolation in the vast mansion. All of a sudden, one of the hallway's light bulbs send out its final light and said goodbye to the world with a sharp popping sound. A few gasps were heard and Amanda even let out a faint scream. The stunned group moved as one down the narrow corridor.

'And darkness fell upon the earth,' Uncle Thomas murmured, taking his wife Georgia into his embrace.

Katerina and Christina rushed down first. They ran into the kitchen and informed the cook that the guests were on their way down.

Mrs Voula, a large woman in her late fifties wiped away the single tear hanging from her eye and rolled up her white sleeves.

'Everything is in the ovens. Nice and warm. Get serving girls,' she said, trying hard to detach her mind from losing her employer. Mrs Zampetaki might have been stiff to most of her employees, but never towards her. Thirty-one years she had cooked for the family and she enjoyed every minute of it. Until today came into existence and death after death brought shock to the household.

The candles in the dining room had remained lit and in the entire room an aroma of wild roses and vanilla flowed through the air. The brightly-colored table with the shiny porcelain plates and a plethora of salads were in full contrast to the gloomy, dark shadowed faces that sat around it. With breakfast interrupted and no lunch served, hunger easily beat out sorrow and guilt. Reluctantly at first, people started to place salad and olive oil coated pita bread on their plates. By the time, the golden grilled chickens came out, surrounded by juicy stuffed vine leaves and oven cooked potatoes and carrots, everyone was eating. Conversations, though quiet ones, had even began.

The tragic figure of Cosma sat at the end of the table; his sister first on his right and Homer first to his left. None of them spoke all evening.

'My God, will the rain ever stop?' Kallisto asked, not being able to bear the silence a minute longer.

'It's really bad out there...' George began to say.

'It's not great in here, either,' Melissa interrupted him. George smiled at her, lifting his hand and gently stroking her hair. 'I'm sorry, baby.'

'For what?'

'For inviting you to the wedding and bringing you in on all this.'

'It's not like you knew what would happen.'

'We could have checked the weather forecast better,' Leonida found the courage to joke.

Beside the two couples, Jenny whispered to the rest of the girls, how her aunt had committed suicide by pills, too.

Further down Ioli's parents sat next to her uncle Thomas and his wife Georgia. 'I never understood people who took their own life,' Gianni said, to receive Anna's notorious disapproving look with the dipping eyebrows and the wide eyes.

'Gianni, not now,' was all she had to say to keep her husband quiet.

Opposite them, Jason was whispering into Mark's ear.

'I'm never going to get laid now.'

'Dude, seriously. Come on.'

'What? That group of ladies was eating out of my palm. I was gonna make a move on the red head tonight and...'

'And a suicide ruined it for you. Boo hoo, malaka.'

'You're one to speak. I've seen how you look at my cousin.'

'Who? Ioli? No, it was just nice to see her after all this time and...'

'Shut up, you're wasting oxygen and persuading no one. If you want my opinion, go for it. She's been single too long. My parents are always going on about her rough life and how she needs a good man to help her move on.'

'Aw, man. That's sweet. You think I am a good man,' Mark said, fighting back a smile and leaning towards Jason.

'Don't get fucking soft with me,' Jason said and pushed Mark off his shoulder.

Jason's mother, Cleopatra turned around and clearly aggravated with him, said 'Boy, just eat and keep quiet.' Cleopatra, a tall, beautiful sixty year old, could not accept the fact that Cassandra had died. Just yesterday, her dreams for her son had come true. He had grown up to be a sensitive, smart, handsome gentleman; he had finished university and had met a terrific girl to spend the rest of his life with. And to top everything, both wanted children. Mother-figure Cleopatra longed to have little ones running around once again. Her husband, Aristo held his wife's trembling hand, while with his other he stroked Homer's back.

'Eat something, you need your strength.'

'For what, dad? To cry on a full stomach?' Homer snapped.

Cleopatra's hands were not the only hands shaking in the room. Little rattles of silverware echoed every now and then behind us. Both girls, Katerina and Christina, served dinned with ashen, distraught faces. Ioli's eyes never left them. She seemed preoccupied with devouring her juicy, well-cooked steak, but I knew better. She loved food, but she loved investigating more.

My attention raced around the table, my ears dropping in and my eyes monitoring movements. *Who could have killed Irene Zampetaki?*

'I know what you're doing, Costa, but you are going to talk to everyone soon. Can I please have some of your attention? I know, this isn't the time for our romantic getaway, yet it would be nice to, at least, feel you close at dinner time,' Tracy quietly said, leaning nearer to my ear. She was right. For her, Irene committed suicide. She saw no reason in me, spying on the guests.

Tracy covered her mouth, choking down the laughter being born inside her, as I turned and smiled at her. A wide smile with gravy-covered lips and teeth decorated with mint and roast beef.

'You're one messy eater, Captain Papacosta! Maybe you should try eating and looking at your plate at the same time.'

'Admit it. You're resisting the urge to kiss me.'

'Costa, stop it, please. If I laugh out, it will be distasteful.'

It would have been a fun, romantic dinner date, but life never goes as planned. Tracy and I sat with a murderer. My eyes once again travelled around the table.

Who could have killed Irene Zampetaki?

Chapter 10

Athens, years ago

Achilles wore his best pair of blue jeans, a black, leather jacket zipped to the top and his trademark goofy smile as he zigzagged amongst the morning bus's passengers. He smiled as he thought that the last time he felt so crowded and confined was when his uncle's sheep were gathered to be sheared. He politely pushed himself through the wall of sleepy students and angry-at-Monday folk who unwillingly said goodbye to the weekend and welcomed another abrupt wake up and journey to work. Achilles normally walked to university. His school stood only a ten minute walk away from his underground home, yet today he rode the bus. A pretty blonde had caught his eye. He knew he had to meet her and he watched as she boarded the 'begging for a wash' bus.

Agatha stood by the window; she always did. The scenery outside was ever changing. New shops opened, different clothes were worn by the same people, flowers bloomed and died, unexpected events took place, and Agatha's eyes devoured it all. Soon after her arrival, she realized this was the place for her. She had fallen in love with noisy, smoky, multi-cultural Athens with its many options of living; the sights, the theatre, and the night clubs. Even the manic, fast-living and often rude people of Athens had started to grow on her.

'Excuse me, I'm so sorry, I am such a mindless fool on Monday morning,' the handsome boy with the short, spiky hair rushed to say.

'It's okay, I'm fine,' Agatha said, though slightly annoyed by her new Louboutin shoes being stepped on. The commercial-white smile she received helped forget the annoyance.

'I was dazzled by your beauty and...'

Agatha could not help but laugh out loud. Her boisterous, cheery laughter embarrassed the young boy, making his green eyes ping-pong side to side to check that the entire bus was not focused on them.

'Cheesy pick up line?'

'The cheesiest,' Agatha said, pushing her long blond hair back.

'Yet true,' Achilles replied, looking straight into her eyes, causing Agatha's high cheekbones to turn a rosy shade of red.

'First year here?' Agatha asked, lowering her eyes.

'How do you know I am not from here?'

'Your dark-colored skin, your genuine smile, your awkward flirting on the morning bus. You're not Athenian for sure, and at your age, I can only guess student.'

'Beauty and brains.'

'Wow, this is turning into a cheese fest,' Agatha replied, giggling.

'It's working, isn't it?'

'How do you know that?'

'For one, you are still talking to me. Secondly, your eyes can't stay away from mine. Anyway, I'm Achilles.'

'Agatha,' she said, extending her hand. Achilles took it gently into his and bowed to kiss it.

'Smooth, country boy. Pretty smooth,' Agatha nodded. 'So, where are you from?'

'Crete...'

'No way,' Agatha's voice climbed the decibel scale. 'Really?'

'Yeah, why so surprised?'

'Me, too. From Chania,' Agatha answered, while her whole face lit up. She hadn't met many people yet; friends were hard to come by. Achilles was the first boy that spoke to her for more than five minutes and about something different than notes from class.

'Young people flirt funny,' an old man sitting in front of them in a brown suit commented to his wife.

'At least they are still flirting,' his white haired wife with the trembling hands replied.

Agatha had loosened her grip from the railing while Achilles did not hold on at all. Both were lost in conversation. The bus driver slammed down the brakes at the next stop due to a skinny, homeless dog sleeping in the bus lane. Both young students fell back onto the glass window, Achilles landing in Agatha's arms.

'They do more than us on a first date, that's for sure,' the old man said and his wife placed a kiss on his cheek while producing screeching laughter.

'I'm sorry...'

'Apologizing again?' Agatha said. 'Oh, shit, it's my stop,' she continued and rushed for the closing doors. Achilles got up and ran behind her, managing to leap off the bus just in time.

Agatha turned around, her hair lifted by the bus-lifted, smoky air. 'You get off here, too?'

'Erm, no. I'm in Med School. Next stop down. But, you're worth missing a lesson or two.'

'Do your smooth lines always work with girls?'

'Yes... I mean no, I...'

'Watch it there, doc. You might hurt yourself.'

'So, architecture, huh?'

'Yep. I want to design big, strange buildings. Watch something grow and be created before my eyes. Leave something behind, you know?'

'My grandmother always said that about trees. She would say it whenever she planted a seed. *This is not for me, it is for you and generations to come*,' he mimicked her voice.

Agatha could not resist but giggle. Humor always won her over with people. *A funny guy has a colorful heart,* her aunt had told her over Easter dinner. She could not remember why.

'You look pretty when you laugh.'

'Compared to the rest of the time when I look ugly?'

'I... No... I meant...'

'I'm joking. Loosen up, doc. And just because you're set on skipping class, does not mean I wish to. So, are you coming?'

'Where?'

'To class, silly. Come on,' she said and took him by his hand.

Achilles ran with her into the dull grey building. *Not much of a place for architects*, he thought. *But hey, at least, I succeeded at meeting her. Dad will be pleased.*

Chapter 11

The grey sky turned black. A 'rock of an island' stood alone in the vast, dark, vicious sea. The menacing clouds devoured the stars and the moon, and darkness prevailed over the land. The power had once again failed the island's inhabitants and light only existed in the Zampetaki mansion due to gas-fueled generators. Their not-so-subtle sound thankfully was not able to reach the library where Ioli and I set up for a fun evening of interrogation.

A long, narrow room, the library boasted countless, large, encyclopaedias and various books categorized into genres. Your classic globe sphere of the earth which opened into a mini bar stood in the corner, while tall-back armchairs were scattered around the room. The ceiling was painted blue in an attempt to resemble the sky, an attempt ruined by the larger-than-life chandeliers.

'Let's prepare our room,' Ioli said, pulling a wooden desk to the center of the room. 'Thank God, they left one room without the entire floor being carpeted,' she said as she pulled the desk past the only carpet of the room.

'Thank God for your muscles. If I pulled that my back would be killing me right now,' I commented, as I pushed two chairs behind the heavy desk.

'You really should check that out, boss. I know I tease you about it a lot, but you're not that old.'

'*That* old?' I asked with a grin, and pulled one more chair to the other side of the desk. I placed my pocket-pen on the table and took out my little, black notebook. Ioli placed her jacket on the chair's back and took out a pack of Jelly Babies, pretzel sticks and a pack of strawberry flavored chewy gums from the inside pocket. Noticing my stare, she smiled.

'What you amazed by? You should know me by now, partner.'

'Oh, I do. You need no pen because you have an eidetic memory and you get hungry easier than a lion during hunting season. Oh, I get you. It doesn't mean it ceases to amaze me.'

A knock grabbed our attention and turned our heads towards the door. We had decided to keep things as casual as possible. We left dinner early and informed everyone to come one by one to the library to give a statement. In any order they preferred. I recommended passing by, just before heading up to bed. That way, they could continue eating and drinking, which would keep them preoccupied, rather than sitting outside the library door.

Cosma's head popped in.

'Cosma. Come in,' I said, in a friendly tone.

'Err, it's not for me. I brought my mother. I was taking her up to bed and she insisted she come. I told her there was no need, yet she does not want to be the odd one out.'

'Stop mumbling, boy! And close the door behind me,' Helena Zampetaki's strong voice ordered him. A mother will always be a mother, never mind how much you grow. My thoughts travelled back to New York and my own mother, now a widow and with an ungrateful son who always keeps forgetting to call as he promised.

Helena Zampetaki marched up to the chair, quite speedily for a woman with a cane. She slowly sat down and placed her olive-wood cane by her side.

'I was in my room during both incidents.' She spoke loud and clear, her wary eyes focused on us. 'Now that's out the way, I wish to discuss ways to keep all this out of the papers. Is there any way we could say Irene went from a broken heart? A heart attack is not uncommon for a woman her age. Suicide is quite the scandal and against our religion, too! I will not have anyone bad-mouthing my precious Irene.'

'With all due respect, ma'am, we cannot lie. And to be frank, the scandal's going to be the murder of the bride, don't you think?' Ioli asked.

'Yes, but that is murder, not blasphemy.'

'Religion is not what it used to be, grandma. I doubt people will be so harsh to condemn Irene to hell just because she committed suicide out of grief for her loss,' Ioli said, leaning forward in her soft armchair and placing her arms upon her legs.

'I can't stand the thought of Irene not being buried inside the cemetery. And don't underestimate religion, child. The devil himself is at play here, have no doubt. What we need is to get rid of the evil eye. I'm telling you, someone is targeting our family and I'm worried about who will be next,' the old lady said, in a steady voice.

'Evil eye? Ma'am, again with all due respect, no one has placed a curse on the family.'

'Find who wants to hurt us and quick,' she demanded and with shaking arms, she lifted herself out of the chair. 'Good night, officers. Happy hunting.'

We said no more. We watched the elderly woman stroll through the library as if on a walk in the park. She grabbed the door handle and struggled to pull it open. Cosma, her son, waited outside and helped her exit through the heavy doorway.

'I'll take her up and be straight down,' Cosma said. He received my nod and just as we turned to each other to discuss the senior woman, Kallisto popped in.

She cat-walked towards us, her healthy curves moving side to side in her tight, glittery dress. 'I know I won't be any help, yet I get anxious knowing that I have something I must do and I am just sitting around waiting to do it, if you understand the feeling.' She spoke at a speed that could win the Grand Prix. Her full cherry lips with the red lipstick moved rapidly up and down. 'This is such a lovely room. Has character, right? And, oh my, is that a genuine Forester piano?' she continued, staring at the piano tucked away in the far right corner, next to the balcony window. The piano player view would be breathtaking; the flat island never obscuring the oceanic horizon. The sunsets here must be majestic; now a pitch black sky met a huge layer of thick olive oil, once the turquoise sea. 'Sorry, I tend to ramble when I'm nervous.'

'Why is it that you believe you will be no help to us? We are just asking where everyone was,' I said, while Ioli simultaneously asked 'Why do you feel nervous?'

Kallisto smiled awkwardly. 'It's my character you see. I always prepare my lines before an interview and now...' she said and showed us with her hands.

'You have no reason to be nervous. Just tell us your whereabouts during both incidents,' Ioli said.

'Incidents. I like that word.' She theatrically took a faint breath and stated her whereabouts. 'I left the party with my boyfriend, Leonida, around quarter to twelve and we went straight to bed. We were exhausted and it did not take long before we were off to dreamland. As for the incident with the mother, I was downstairs the entire time. You saw me, you were there,' she said, staring at Ioli who politely smiled back.

'How well did you know Cassandra?' I asked.

'Not that well. I only met her once back in the States and she seemed a lovely girl. Homer had sorted out a little get together with his cousin. We went wine tasting. It was splendid. Oh, there I go blabbing again. I was going to do her make-up for the big day and we did a couple of rehearsals that day. She was so polite and kind,' Kallisto said, and wiped the corner of her eye. Her long nails so close to her eye made my shoulders shiver. I never could stand people touching or rubbing their eyes. Watching someone place their contacts in was among the scariest things I have ever witnessed.

'You were going to do her makeup?' Ioli wondered. 'No offense, it's just that a rich girl like Cassandra could have had any professional makeup artist she pleased.'

'I am a professional,' Kallisto retaliated. 'That's how I started out. I did the makeup for the actors before the show, before I became a star myself. I was pretty good, if I may say so myself. I was so good that many questioned if it was a good idea to give it up and became an actress. My mother knew I was making good money and did not want me to be an actress.'

'Must have been a difficult decision for you,' Ioli said, failing to hide the sarcasm in her tone. Kallisto looked straight at her.

'There are no difficult decisions in life, my dear. When you throw up a coin in the air, you always know on which side you really want it to land.'

Just then, the door opened and the tragic figure of a broken man walked in.

'Oh, I'm sorry, I did not realize that...' Cosma began to say and turned to leave.

'No, no. Stay. I am just chatting away, eating up these peoples' precious time.' Kallisto stood up and gave the armchair to Cosma. 'My condolences,' she said as she sat him down and cat-walked back out of the room, her hands in her red purse, searching for her thin, stick-like cigarettes.

I looked at Cosma. All color had left him. He seemed to have grown a decade older in the last day. It is times like this I wished I still smoked. He kept his swollen, red eyes low. He played with his fingers the whole time he sat in front of us.

'Mr Zampetaki, I'm not even going to pretend to comprehend what you are going through at the moment, but I'm going to need you to bear with me here. Let's say for argument's sake that the old lady had an accomplice. Who in the house would you consider it to be?' Ioli took no time to head to the point.

His eyes open wide; his strong jaw dropped a few inches and shook as he spoke.

'You believe she had an accomplice?' he asked.

'Just a possibility we have to examine, sir. She was a very old and fragile lady. Seems a bit difficult to imagine her pulling this off alone,' Ioli replied, deliberately leaving out words about murder, slicing of the throat and stabbing in the back.

'I can't think of anyone here that could be connected to the vendetta. Everyone here is family of mine and Homer's or friends from America.'

'What about your personnel?' I asked.

'We run background checks on all our staff -house, office and winery. We would never hire anyone related to that horrid family. Besides, everyone loved Cassandra,' he said, choking on her name. 'She was such a lovely girl. So happy all the time...' His eyes fell to the floor; his head shaking with sorrow.

'Cosma, indulge me with the next few questions, and try to not read so much into them.'

He lifted up his head slowly, as if sedated; his eyes revealing his inner curiosity building up. He nodded with difficulty.

'Who benefits from your wife's will?'

He smiled at the question. 'I feel like I am on one of those shows. You know, the investigative cop ones. The husband is always the prime suspect and I guess I would be when I disclose that everything goes to me. However, my wife committed suicide and my daughter had nothing to her name.'

'Everything? Sorry for asking for details, but if they is a relative or a friend you included in your will...'

'No, no. We had no wills.'

'No wills? I find that a bit difficult to believe. You are a prosperous, wealthy family and...'

'This is not America, Captain. We have no need for a will. By Greek law, everything you own automatically goes to your spouse and if your spouse is deceased, everything goes to your children, in equal shares.'

Ioli leaned forward, placed her hands on the glass surface of the wooden desk and asked 'In case of your death who inherits the estate?' .

Cosma remained silent for a whole minute. Ioli stared at me, raising her eyebrows.

'In a matter of a day, I went from being a married man with a daughter ready to marry and provide me with grandchildren, to being a childless widow,' Cosma finally spoke. 'I guess it would go to my sister, Anneta.' He paused for a second.

'Well, my share would at least. Irene has just died. I don't know how long it will take to transfer everything to my name. Maybe if I die, her share would go to her next of kin,' he continued, his voice more of a mumble than addressing us.

'And that would be?' I asked.

'One of her first cousins. She had no siblings and her parents have passed on. You may have noticed, most of the guests are Homer's family. Cassandra wanted a small wedding so Irene did not invite any of her side. They were not that close, really. My wife did not really get along that well with... other people,' he said and smiled fondly.

'How was her relationship with the staff then?' Ioli inquired.

'Oh, I would guess that they rather hated her,' he replied with honesty. 'She was one tough boss, that's for sure. My own 'iron lady' I used to call her.' His face fell into his wrinkled hands and tears were born in the corners of his brown eyes.

I gave him a minute. 'For our report, where were you around midnight last night and during your wife's bath today?' I asked casually, not wanting to hint any sort of blame.

He raised his head and cleared his throat. He quickly wiped away any tears left upon his cheeks. 'Last night, Irene and I left last from the dining room around one o'clock. We were the hosts, we left after everyone had gone up.'

'Who were the last to leave?' Ioli asked.

'Homer's parents, your uncle Thomas and his wife, and your cousin George, with the girl with the burnt face. Sorry, for calling her that. Sounds terrible. I do not recall her name.'

'Melissa,' Ioli helped him out.

'Yes, yes. Melissa. Quiet one she is, yet she stayed up drinking with George. He and Leonida got quite drunk. Leonida kept hugging his cousin and ordering drinks until his girlfriend finally carried him off to bed.'

He sat quietly while both of us stared at him.

'Oh, yes. I forgot,' he apologized, remembering he did not inform us of his whereabouts during his wife's 'suicide'. 'I was in our bedroom. Irene kissed me and said she was going to take a bath.

Christina, our maid, came in to bring her a cup of herbal tea that Irene had ordered. She saw my wife go in the bathroom. I left the room shortly after Christina and went to the TV room on the top floor. My sister Anneta was there, too,' he continued saying as he stared at the floor.

'That's convenient,' Ioli leaned towards me, and whispered.

He was getting ready to cry again. His eyes were watery and his hands began to tremble.

'Thank you, Cosma. That'll be all,' I said with my voice raised.

'No, no. I thank you for doing this. I'm sure the guests would rather speak with you two than the police when they arrive. As soon as the weather settles, I figure everyone will need to rush home and distance themselves from all this,' he said, got up, nodded to us with a slight smile and sauntered out the room.

The bang of the door, signalling our time to talk alone.

'Why did you reveal our suspicions to Cosma? He is a suspect. He acts so distraught, yet did you see how casually he walks around?' I asked.

'What do we have to lose? If he is guilty, it would alert him that we are on to him and maybe force him to do something stupid; a mistake to catch him. If he is innocent, then at least we got answers and warned him to be careful. He could very well be the next murder/suicide. Maybe there will be an accident this time?'

'You're probably right. Just ran it by me so I don't get so caught off guard next time.'

'Sure thing, boss.'

'No one related to that horrid family, he said. Maybe someone paid by them?' I thought out loud.

'I've noted that he, Irene, Thomas, Georgia, George and Melissa were together in the dining room during Cassandra's murder,' Ioli said.

'Still got a long list of suspects to add to your theory that the old lady had an accomplice.'

The knocking on the door silenced us.

'Come in,' I called out.

The room welcomed in George and Melissa. George, smart-looking as always, came in wearing a grey pair of trousers, held up by a designer belt, and a navy blue shirt under his charcoal sweater with the thin white lines running across. His shiny black shoes matched his hair; for a forty-year old, his hair stood unharmed by time. Hollywood hair, Tracy had called it. That was not the only feature he shared with Gary Grant. Deep dimples, youthful skin, engaging eyes and a strong jaw formed his face. Besides him, the 'savaged by fire' face of his girlfriend. Melissa lacked the confidence of women who normally grace the arm of such a fine specimen of a gentleman. She avoided eye contact and you had to struggle just to hear her speak. She dressed plainly, in a long brown skirt and a dark green cardigan on top. I wondered if she had always been shy in her life or the fire had forced her into it. Nevertheless, it did not stop her from finding George, who she seemed to be very much in love with. Always by his side, and touching him at every chance. With a stroke on the cheek, her hand upon his, or her head on his shoulder. Her rock after her ship had sunk.

'Do you mind if we see you together?' George asked.

I shook my head. 'Of course not...'

'Can I come, too? I know you have already spoken to Kallisto. I would hate to get stuck last.' Leonida's head popped in through the open door.

'The more the merrier. Close the door behind you,' Ioli said, as she stood up to fetch a couple more chairs. George rushed to help her, while Leonida sat down in the only armchair opposite us.

George sat in a straight posture between the two and spoke first; the most confident of the three.

'Is Homer OK, Ioli? He hasn't really said a word since Cassandra's death.'

'Under the circumstances, he is holding up, yet, you know Homer. He is just waiting to go somewhere alone and cry his heart out. He acts strong, but inside...'

'Inside we are all in pain,' Melissa completed Ioli's sentence. 'It helps to cry. I lost both my parents and most of my face in a car accident. It's been years since then and I still cry whenever I think of them.'

'It's always hard to lose someone so close to you,' I said. 'Now, you know why we called you all here. We need to note down everybody's whereabouts during the two incidents. That's midnight last night and today afternoon.'

'Well, last night, we left last from the party. What time was it, dear?' George asked Melissa.

'Must have been after one for sure,' she quietly said.

'You?' Ioli asked Leonida.

'I left before midnight with Kallisto. We went straight up to our room. We were exhausted from the trip and after a quick shower we slept like babies. I remember worrying that after a shower and with all the thunder outside, I would not sleep easy, but in a matter of seconds I was out.'

'And today?'

'Today all four of us were in the dining room having drinks,' Leonida replied.

'And none of you left the room?' I asked.

'No,' George replied with a steady voice.

'That is because you were so busy drinking with Leonida to notice me leave,' Melissa said. George turned to face his girlfriend. His eyes were moving around, unsure.

'Oh, don't give me that look,' she fondly said, and stroked his cheek. 'I'm not complaining. I left the room for a while,' she continued, turning towards us. 'But I didn't go upstairs. I needed to use the ladies' room and got carried away admiring the art in the hallway. I strolled all the way down to the kitchen. Christina saw me there. Then, I came straight back to the dining room.'

'So, I guess that is all you need from us then,' Leonida said and stood up. Without waiting for a reply from us, he walked over to the globe situated on a wooden tripod near the first row of bookcases. He flipped the top of the earth open and whistled. 'So, this is where they keep the good stuff,' he said, lifting up a bottle of aged cognac. George rolled his eyes. 'Leonida!'

'What?' Leonida replied. 'We are stuck here. Cosma has lost a daughter and a wife. I'm pretty sure he would not mind us having a drink,' he continued while pouring himself a glass.

'*A* drink,' George answered, emphasizing the A.

'Oh, come on. You're going to lecture me on my drinking, now? Here?'

'I think we should be going. We have wasted enough of their time,' Melissa said to George, her hand caressing his shoulder.

After the trio's departure, it was the maids turn to show up and enter the warm room. Christina, who came in timidly, standing behind rangy Katerina, confirmed Melissa's story. The hollow-cheeked twenty-year old sat down and with chary eyes, carefully listened to Ioli's questions.

'Yes, I spoke with her. She spoke to me about the food. She loves to cook and wanted to know more about the meal that was going to be served,' Christina said.

'Poor woman, with all those nasty scars. She must have been beautiful before the accident. You can tell by the eyes. And she is so kind. At first she seemed distant, but she gives out this gentle soulful feeling. Out of all of the guests, I feel like I know her the best,' Katerina said. 'No offense to the rest of the guests,' she quickly added. 'It's just that most don't bother paying much attention to the *help.*'

'Oh, but we do,' Ioli said. 'I noticed your lovely perfume. Has a very distinct flowery scent, yet leaves you with a touch a lemon afterwards. I like that. The sweet and the bitter together,' my partner said, as if she was talking with her girlfriends in a cafe in Chania.

Katerina's smile widened. 'Really? I was unsure when I bought it.'

'I smelled it in Irene's bathroom, too. Did she have the same?'

The corners of her smile journeyed back down, creating a flat line smile. 'No, no. Mrs Zampetaki would never wear something so cheap.'

'Must have been you, then,' Ioli casually added.

'Yes, I ran her bath for her.'

'Were you there when she entered the room?' I asked.

'No, I was alone. Christina saw her when she brought up her tea.'

My eyes turned in Christina's direction.

'She was in her bathrobe when I brought in the tea. She said she would drink it after her bath and told me to leave it on her bedside table. She then went into the bathroom and locked the door behind her. I then left the room and came straight back down to the kitchen.'

'Closed the door,' Ioli said.

'Huh?' the young girl with the short, curly hair, asked.

'You said *locked* the door. The door was not locked; the key was on the outside.'

The girl looked stunned. 'Yes, you're right,' she murmured, lost in thought.

'So what is it? Locked or closed?' I asked.

'She definitely locked the door behind her. She always does. I heard the key turn.'

'I've been here longer. Christina is right. She absolutely hated it when Mr Zampetaki or the kids interrupted her bath time. It was *her time*, you know?' Katerina backed up Christina's story.

'Woo, woo. Slow down,' I said, my heart beat accelerating to warp speed. 'Kids?'

Both girls looked at each other. Katerina swallowed with difficulty and looked up, fixing her gaze to the corner of the long room. She then lowered her head and even though alone, she whispered to us. 'They had another daughter. She died in that terrible airplane crash. Do you remember the one, years ago? That Olympic flight from Greece to London? She was aboard that plane.'

'So, that's why Anneta mentioned all the daughters lost in this world,' I mumbled.

'Guess riches can't buy you happiness,' Christina said quietly.

'Or armor to protect you from tragedies,' Ioli added. 'Was the Zampetaki family a happy family?' she quickly threw the question, hoping for an honest response.

Katerina sat up uneasy. 'I don't think it is our place to say,' the middle-aged maid said.

'Never really saw any of them ever get along with each other. Sir never spoke to his wife, she only talked to him when she needed him to do something and their daughter only came from her studies in America to visit them once a year and even then, things were cold. Cassandra was such a kind, smiley person and I never saw her once smile at her parents,' Christina announced in a spur of honesty. 'What?' she asked Katerina -who looked at her with a dropped jaw and eyes wide open. 'It's the truth. You know my grandma used to say that the bigger the house, the further apart the people in it and ever since I began working for this family, I realized how wise her words truly were.'

'I see,' Ioli said, while my pen scribbled everything down. 'So, for our report, where were you while Mrs Irene took her bath?'

'Together in our lounge next to the kitchen,' Katerina answered, clearly annoyed by Christina's honesty on the Zampetaki family bonds.

'Anyone else there with you?'

'No, just the two of us,' Christina answered.

'What was on the TV?' I asked.

'Deal or no deal,' both replied in unison.

'And, during the party last night?' Ioli inquired.

'We served drinks and appetizers until everyone left. Then, we stayed up for another hour cleaning up.'

'Together again?' Ioli asked.

'Yes, the two of us,' Katerina asked, the annoyance in her voice coloring each word as it came out her too-small-for-her-long-face mouth.

'Christina,' I addressed the frank, slim girl. 'You discovered Irene Zampetaki's body...'

'Don't remind me.'

I smiled gently. 'You said Mrs Irene locked the door behind her.' She nodded in agreement. 'How did you unlock it?'

'I didn't! The key was on the outside and the door was not locked. I had come up to ask Madame about dinner and when she did not reply, I figured she had left and opened the door to let some air into the bathroom. Mr Zampetaki is always complaining how her steamy baths with the window closed, damage the wall paint.'

'So you opened the door...' Ioli tried to help the girl focus, and return to the story.

'Madame was under water. I screamed and fell back and screamed again. Besides my grandma's body at her funeral, I have never seen a dead body before!' Christina said, her voice becoming shaky.

'Did you go near to her? Check for vital signs?' Ioli asked.

'Are you crazy?' Christina replied, followed by a quick 'sorry.' Ioli waved a no problem. 'All I did was scream, until Mr Zampetaki came.'

'Did he come alone?' I asked. 'Was his sister with him?'

'No, he was alone.'

The awkward moment of silence that followed next, came to an end with a deafening thunder that broke through the sky outside and rain plummeted down heavier, raging down on the mansion.

'That will be all,' I said with a half-smile towards the two women. Both nodded and rushed out of the room. I exhaled deeply.

'Where was his sister if he was with her at the time of death?'

'Can't wait to get Anneta in here. By the way, every cell of my body dislikes Katerina. Every time I speak to her, I get the feeling she is hiding something, or she acts as if someone is listening in and she whispers and behaves secretively,' Ioli said, while stuffing down candy after every other word.

'What if the two murders aren't linked?' I expressed the thought that came to life in my mind.

'What are the chances of that?'

'Well, what if someone took advantage of Cassandra's murder and used it to kill Irene and staged it as a suicide? Nearly everyone saw her try to jump off the cliff.'

'Sounds possible, though my candy-filled gut is screaming that all this is connected,' Ioli said and kept devouring her sweets. She lifted a colorful nylon bag towards my eyes. 'Care for a strawberry flavored teddy bear?'

I declined, as more rain attacked the 'vibrating from the constant thunders' windows. I felt like the mansion was trying to shake itself to death. The winds grew ferocious and brought chaos to the world outside. The noise of loose garden ornaments rolling by the pool side and smashing against the brick garden wall blocked out the faint knocking at the door. A heavier knock followed.

'Now that's how you knock,' Thomas's deep voice said, and chuckled.

'Let's just get this over and done with,' Gianni's spoke up, and covered Thomas's childish laughter.

'Boys, behave,' Georgia said and knocked again. Anna just rolled her eyes.

Inside, Ioli did the same. 'Oh, no. My family is here. Great. Get ready for four people talking all at the same time and correcting each other incessantly on mindless details.'

To be honest, she wasn't entirely wrong.

It took the group of four a while to agree upon the time they left the dinner party, ranging from eleven something to one o'clock.

'I went up first around eleven,' Anna said.

'No, it was later than that,' her husband corrected her.

'What time did you come up, then?' she asked him.

'I came up behind Homer and the poor girl. Before midnight... I think.'

'We left just after midnight, didn't we?' Georgia said, asking her husband.

'No, it was closer to one,' Thomas replied.

At least, they agreed that they were all together next to the fireplace with Ioli during Irene's suicide.

'That poor, tormented woman...' Anna began her well-known monologue upon hearing a tragedy.

'Mama, not now,' Ioli cut her off.

'Don't interrupt your mother with that tone,' Gianni told her off.

'Can we just arrest him?' Ioli asked, turning towards me. 'You can be on your way, thank you,' she continued. 'We have many people to see.'

'Have you eaten something sweet, dear? You seem agitated...' Anna began to say, only to be cut off again by a strong 'Mama!' and an ice-cold glare. The four sixty-plus year olds were still discussing the time as they exited the room, leaving the door wide open. We did not speak between us. We sat and watched the open door. It's a strange feeling anticipating, guessing who will be next. A shadowy figure appeared in the dark hallway and slowly approached the well-lit room. Homer closed the door behind him, and with an expressionless face came and sat before us.

His broad back filled the tall back armchair while his awkwardness pervaded the high-ceiling room. He stared around at the rows of well-maintained and dustless books.

'Never been in here before?' I asked.

'Oh, no. I have. Cassie gave me the grand tour on our first day here.'

'How are you coping?' Ioli asked.

He raised his shoulders and lifted his hands. 'I have no comparison, but I guess I am as I expected to be,' he enigmatically replied, while a strong whiff of whiskey floated in the air as he spoke.

Ioli accepted his answer with a half-smile and moved on. 'On the night of Cassandra's murder, you stated that you were together until sometime after midnight when you said your goodbyes and you went straight to bed.'

'Yes, we wanted to be fresh for our wedding day. Why the hell did she go out into the storm to try on her dress...?' Homer's voice grew stronger, he clenched his fists and his breathing became heavier.

'Where were you during Irene's suicide? You did not come down at all since lunch,' Ioli continued.

'Did not feel like being around people much. Stayed upstairs, flicked through cable TV, played with my phone...'

'Anyone that can verify this?' I asked.

Homer straightened up, his head tilting to one side. He looked straight at me. 'Why does someone need an alibi for a suicide?'

'Why don't you just answer the question?' Ioli calmly advised.

'My parents. They kept on coming in and out, checking on me and my dad sat with me for most of the time. There was a documentary about how the brain functions. He loves shit like that.'

Ioli watched as I scribbled down to verify with his parents and asked him about Cassandra's relationship with her parents.

'Weird.'

'In what way?'

'When I met Cassie, she never mentioned them and even when the conversation turned to our families and roots, she would always talk about other members of her family and change the subject on the first chance. It was kind of like she was... disgusted by them, somehow.'

'Disgusted?'

'Yes, as if she wanted nothing to do with them. I always believed she was an estranged daughter. I mean, she never even called them. Greeks in America are always on the phone with their parents. Yet, when I proposed and we decided on our families to meet, she held no argument. Imagine my surprise when I met them and they were over the moon in love with their daughter. They did everything for us, offered to pay for everything. Whenever Cosmas and Irene were with their daughter, they were all over her. Holding her hand, asking her how were things and about her life in general. She had starved them for her attention.'

'And how did Cassandra react to all this attention?' Ioli asked.

Homer looked at his cousin and lowered his eyes. 'To be honest with you, Ioli, she remained as cold as ever with them. I know how bad it sounds, but I had started to think she was some sort of gold digger that agreed to speak with her parents again just to use their money for the wedding. They flew us all over and today the ferry was supposed to bring over all her friends from Chania. All paid for, the bus and the ferry. They were going to buy us a house in Chania, too. She was their only child and everything they owned was hers, Cosmas often told her.'

'Did she ever speak about her sister?' I inquired.

'Not really. Mostly when recalling childhood memories. It was a difficult subject for her, always bringing tears to her eyes. It sounded like they were close as children.'

'Thank you, Homer,' I said in my tone of *you may excuse yourself now*.

'I'll send in my parents,' he said, stood up, wiped the few droplets of sweat from his forehead and with a fast pace, he exited the snug room. The central heating of the old house worked fine and soon, I removed my jacket, having first checked my shirt's armpits for unwanted pools. There is nothing worse than trying to read a suspect's eyes, while they stare at your sweaty patches. The large windows fogged up due to the contrast of temperature in the library and that of the icy cataclysm outside.

Aristo and Cleopatra Cara entered the room. Cleopatra walked straight towards us, while Aristo closed the door. Both wore expressions of sadness and sorrow upon their faces. We already knew that they were still at the dinner party during Cassandra's murder so Ioli shot straight to the point.

'Uncle, auntie,' she began her questions by addressing them, 'why didn't you come down today? Did you stay in your room all day?'

Her uncle, Aristo, sat up. 'Come down for what? Our son was locked in his room, crying over his dead bride. Were we supposed to come down and smile at everyone?'

'Besides, I wasn't feeling so well, dear. A bit under the weather. I think the storm has brought me a nice cold,' Cleopatra added with her fragile voice fighting to be heard.

'Locked in his room? You did not see him?'

'Of course we did!' Aristo raised his voice. 'It's just an expression. Locked in his room. We went over often to check up on him; we're his parents!'

'Brain function documentary kept him busy, huh?' Ioli asked casually.

'Yes, yes. Quite interesting, I must say.'

After a few questions of mine about them noticing anything suspicious or seeing Cassandra leave the house, the pair got up and left the room. Ioli sat quietly during my questions. As the door remained open and Anneta appeared in the wooden doorway, Ioli stood up, mumbled a sorry and walked straight past her and out of the room.

'Sit down,' I said and pointed out the upholstered armchair to Anneta.

'I would say good evening, but this is anything but that.'

In the hallway, Ioli caught up with her uncle and aunt. She passed them and stood in front of them.

'Did we forget something, dear?' Cleopatra asked.

Ioli's eyes scanned around to make sure no other ears were to be found.

'Yes, you forgot to tell the truth,' she said with a steady voice.

'How dare you say we lied? What kind of family...' Aristo began his rant.

His wife placed her hand upon him and whispered a 'shh.'

'Ioli, why do you say such a thing?'

'Aunt Cleo, I notice when perfect strangers lie to me, never mind you two, who I grew up watching. Aristo's eyes wobble when he lies and you always look down and play with your thumb. What I don't know is why you felt that you needed to lie.'

Cleopatra exhaled and pushed her hair back with both hands. 'Homer asked us to.'

'Cleo!' her husband cut her off. She raised her hand towards him and continued explaining to Ioli. 'It's only a half lie. We did check up on him and he was in his room, but he wanted to be alone, so we returned to our room and I fell asleep while Aristo watched TV. When you asked to see us all, Homer asked his father to say that they were together watching TV.'

'But why?'

'I know, right? I told them it was silly. You need no alibi for a suicide, but as you know neither of them ever listen to me,' she said and shook her head, while calling to Saint Mary to provide them with sense.

As Ioli attempted to make sense outside, Anneta approached and sat down. She looked refreshed, during dinner she looked like all blood had been drained out of her plum shaped body. Her hair had been blown dry and an eighties style had come alive. She had even slipped out of her ankle length black dress and changed into a knee high black skirt with a peach blouse, designed perfectly to cover the extra kilos gathered around her waist. She took her time to approach, her eyes studying the room. 'Sorry, it has been a while since I have been in here. I love this room's architecture. See, how the marble columns bend towards the top?'

I nodded and watched her make herself comfortable before I began my set of questions.

'I left the party rather early,' she answered my first question. 'I have never been one for staying up late. By eleven, I must have been fast asleep.'

'And during Irene's suicide?'

'I was with my brother. I'm sure he told you that.'

'Was Mega channel showing the game today?'

The lines on her forehead met and pointed down towards her widened eyes. She tilted her head to the left and replied 'I do not observe sports, Captain.'

'I see. What did you watch then?'

'I didn't...' she began to say, and then stopped. She studied me for a second. 'Just had the TV on, for noise. I really only paid attention to the evening news.'

'Anything interesting in the world?'

'Depends on what you find to be interesting.'

'And your brother did not want to watch the game?'

'I know men can be men, but he just lost his wife after losing his daughter. Sports were the last thing on his mind.'

My fingers intertwined and I leaned forward. 'And when Cosmas heard the screams of Christina and rushed down to find his drowned wife, where were you?'

'I had just got up to go find my book. As I said, TV is not really my thing.'

'And you did not hear the screams?'

She lowered her eyes. 'Well, I must have been in the ladies room at that moment. My hearing is not very good, I must admit. Then, I picked up my book from my bedside table and walked back to where I'd left my brother. He was not there, so I walked towards the staircase and that is when I saw the people running towards Irene's room.'

'What book are you reading?' I asked, never changing my expression.

'Just a silly romance novel you would never have heard of.'

'That's true. Sci-fi is more my thing.'

'Sci-fi? Breaking the cliché of detective novels?'

'I have enough detective stories in real life. I read to escape.'

'Guess it is the same with me and romance novels. I read about what I don't have,' she admitted softly, in a moment of honesty. Then, she blushed and her eyes shot straight to the Persian carpet. 'Sorry, I...'

'No need,' I waved my hand. 'You never married? If I may take the liberty and ask?'

'Oh, there was a boy once. A classic tale of finding love and having your young heart so ripped out of your chest that you knew, even then, that you would never truly love again.'

'As a man who has lost at love and won it back, my only advice is never give up. Love has its way to work things out.'

'You are sure, you don't read romance novels?' she asked with a half-smile and without waiting for a reply, she added 'I better be going. I believe you'll have a long night ahead of you.'

I wished her a good night and my eyes followed her out of the room. I was puzzled by Anneta. Her story did not register well in the analytical parts of my brain, though she spoke her words as if utter truth. I span round my office chair towards the window and gazed at the chaos outside. I enjoyed the rain more than your average Joe, but this storm did not give birth to the sense of freedom and nirvana that most rains brought to me. I stood up and rubbed my lower back. I scanned the room 360 degrees; I was alone. I stretched my arms up and tip toed until the pain from my back began to fade. I, then, fixed my boxer shorts. How they manage to always journey up and crawl around my privates will always be an unsolved mystery. I strolled towards the window, wishing I could open it and smell the fresh air.

'Wanna open the huge window during a storm?' Ioli asked as she re-entered the room.

'Reading my mind again?'

'What did the sister have to stay?' Ioli asked, as she walked to my side.

'Not much really. Covered for her brother. Backed his story about watching TV together.'

'Then why did she come down ten minutes after he did?'

'Bad hearing. Ladies room. Locating a book. I heard it all,' I said and chuckled with a grin across my tired face. 'You? What took you so long?'

'My uncle and aunt were covering for Homer. He asked them to so, so I went and found him.'

'And?'

'He said that he *felt* that something suspicious was up, and was worried because he thought everyone was down in the dining room together. He said that he panicked thinking how it would look. His exact words were 'bereaved fiancé murders mother-in-law for a vendetta that took his wife-to-be away.'

'Felt?'

'I know, right? Bullshit. And Anneta covering her brother and that Katerina always worried about saying the wrong thing? These people know it was not a suicide.'

Just then the lights grew strong and then with a buzz and a crack went dead. The mansion's power vanished in a second, darkening the house. Pitch black filled the vast rooms and brought panic into people's hearts.

Voices grew louder, hands searched around for flashlights and candles, while others held up their phones providing light.

Ioli's phone came equipped with a flashlight and a small circle of light came to life on the wildly patterned Persian carpet. I placed my right hand upon her shoulder and followed her out of the room. Most guests had gathered in the front hall.

'I thought the island had its own power source now?' Uncle Thomas said.

Cosmas stood in the midst of them, explaining that it does and that the power cut was most likely due to the raging storm. 'We have two powerful generators. Nothing to worry about. Katerina is on her way down to turn them on.'

'Why don't you have security back-up so the motors come on...' Jason began his usual complaining; only to be cut off by gasping screams coming from the main stairwell. Flashlights, candles and cell phones pointed towards the direction of the female voice only to reveal a tumbling down the stairs Anneta. Her hands were trying to grab on to the marble railing, but in vain. Apparently, her right high heel had broken off throwing her down the steps, head first to the ground.

'Oh, God,' Cosmas yelled, seeing his sister lying on the floor with her eyes closed and blood dripping from her forehead.

'Anneta! Anneta!' he yelled, taking her head into his arms.

'Don't move her,' Mark ordered as he came down the stairs, aided by Christina who carried a strong flashlight. The group of four bridesmaids followed behind them.

Cosmas obeyed and gently lowered his sister's bleeding head back to the ground.

'This is the house of horrors,' Georgia whispered to Anna, who held on to her rock, Gianni, with her left hand while crossing herself with her right.

'May the Lord help us all,' Anna managed to say.

'Told you. It's the bad eye,' Helena Zampetaki turned and said to me.

Ioli rushed over to Mark, who knelt beside Anneta's unconscious body.

'Is she OK?' she asked as the light came back to life. Sighs of relief spread throughout the room.

Mark smiled towards her while giving orders to Christina to bring essentials from the kitchen and Jason to bring his first aid kit from upstairs.

'She is going to need stitches,' he said, facing Ioli with a calm look upon his face. 'She will be fine,' he assured Cosma, having checked Anneta's vital signs.

There are three types of people when it comes to blood and cuts. Most turned away as Mark washed Anneta's wound with pure alcohol and prepared his needle. Some looked for a split second and then turned away with a shiver. And then, you have those you watch on with a peculiar expression across their face. Normally, these are people who have or feel like they have, seen it all. Ioli and I did not turn away, her father, Gianni, did not, Jason looked on with a proud expression for his friend, the doctor. Helena Zampetaki even came closer to see. The rest had their heads lowered or turned in another direction. That is when I noticed, Alexandra's eyes steadily fixed on the needle penetrating Anneta's skin. The tallest of the four bridesmaids she watched on as the other three quivered away from the sight.

Anneta's eyelids flickered and slowly journeyed upwards to reveal her stunned honey colored eyes. Mark and Ioli helped her to sit up and lean back onto the magnolia painted wall. Disoriented and in pain, Anneta asked for some water.

'Is she okay?' Cosma's worried voice repeated behind them.

'She will be fine,' Mark replied, raising his voice. 'Just be quiet and let her relax for a minute.

Katerina came flying into the room, water-filled glass in trembling hand. Ioli assisted Anneta with drinking it and as the distraught woman gulped down the last sip, she opened her eyes wide.

'You!' she yelled, staring right at Mark. 'Was it you?' she asked and then turned and lifted her head towards Christina. 'Or you?'

'Ma'am, please calm down...' Mark began to say.

'Don't you ma'am me. I saw you two talking on the stairwell, I walked straight pass you and then the lights went out and I was pushed!'

'Pushed?' Cosmas repeated in shock.

'No, no. We did not push you,' Mark said, his eyes travelling from Anneta to Ioli. 'Why on earth would we push you?'

'Sir, I swear. I never even went near your sister. The lights went out and I went to fetch the flashlights and...' Christina produced ten words per second, excusing herself to her employer.

Anna crossed herself again and even uttered an 'oh, my God. Jesus save us' as grandma Zampetaki said that someone was trying to kill them all. 'A demon is among us,' the old lady continued.

Tracy, who so far sat quietly on a chair tucked away next to a Hellenic Apollo statue, stood up and approached me. She hugged me from behind and placed her head upon my back. She needed to feel safe. I turned around and took her into my arms, leaving Ioli to deal with Anneta.

'Anneta, are you sure someone pushed you?' You could have tripped. It was dark...' Ioli calmly spoke to the heavily breathing woman.

'I... I... don't know. As I fell, I remember thinking that I was pushed, but to be honest, I do not recall anyone touching me,' she said and her right hand held her head. She squinted her eyes in obvious pain.

'You have taken a pretty severe hit. I fear a concussion. You need to lie down and stay there. I will check up on you until the storm passes. You need to get to a hospital,' Mark said, giving his best shot at a smile.

'You are so kind, and all I have done is accuse you of throwing me down the stairs...'

'No worries. Doctor's orders. Now, let's get you to bed.'

'Bet it has been a while since she last heard that from a man,' Jason joked, whispering into Amanda's ear. Amanda's plump cheeks pinked up as she resisted a giggle.

'Talking about the storm, had anyone had any updates on when the ferries will be up and running again?' Cleopatra asked.

'Tomorrow is a definite no,' Leonidas said, standing hand in hand with Kallisto. 'I spoke with the ferry company just a few hours ago.'

'That's a shame,' Thomas added. 'Though on the news it said that after tomorrow the weather should start clearing up.'

'Let's pray for that, then,' Kallisto replied, to receive smiles and nods from the group.

Ioli and Mark had already begun ascending the stairs with frail Anneta hanging between them. Cosmas followed behind, ashen and with worried eyes. He paused and turned towards the crowd, focusing his eyes on me. 'Maybe we shall call it a night?'

I wanted to reply no, having already questioned most of the house's occupants, however a look at the tired, distraught, confused faces around me, forced to reply with a simple 'Yes, sure, no problem. We'll pick up tomorrow from when we left off.'

Upstairs, in her spacious guest room with the two beds and the separate sitting area, Anneta exhaled deeply as Ioli and Mark helped her into her king-sized bed with the floral covers.

'Now, get some rest and if you need anything, don't hesitate to call,' Mark said in his professional tone of voice.

'Could you be as kind to close the curtains for me?' Anneta breathlessly asked. 'I cannot stand looking at this storm any longer,' she added, her eyes focused on the wet windows. Through the multiple droplets residing on the glass, a grey world unfolded, a world ravished by winds and rain.

'Of course,' Ioli said, and closed the heavy drapes. The darkness of the room grew deeper and all light gathered around Anneta's night light.

'Again, sorry and thank you,' Anneta said, her eyes fixed on Mark.

'No need.' He waved his hand and with a gentle smile, he turned to leave. Ioli followed him, closing the door behind her. The rattling of the door handle gave the signal for Anneta's eyelids to descend. Soon, she drifted off to sleep.

'Another shitty day in paradise,' Mark said, with an awkward half smile.

'Pretty much so,' Ioli responded and turned to come find me.

'Don't,' Mark said and grabbed her hand. He brought it into his and stroked it with his soft fingers.

'Mark..., I...'

'Sorry for being so straight forward, but it is killing me inside. I can't keep my eyes off you and you are always in my sight and people keep dying around us and getting hurt and yes, it's sad and fucked up and all, but what pissed me off the most is that it is keeping me from talking to you and...'

'That's a lot of *ands* in your sentence. May I lend you a full stop for a minute?'

Mark chuckled. 'Cliché kind of guy. Strong, silent type and when I decide to finally speak, I sound like a teenage girl talking to her high school crush.'

Ioli pushed back her black hair and slightly licked her upper lip. 'Mark, this is not the time nor the place...'

'More clichés,' he interrupted.

'Clichés become clichés for a reason. And if all this is not a perfect fit for the wrong time, wrong place cliché, I don't know what is. Please, don't get me wrong. Don't take this as a cold hearted no. See it as a professional rule. Don't mix business with pleasure. Is that a cliché too?'

'I think it falls more into the lines of a saying.'

'Weird things are going on and until things are resolved, I am definitely not getting close to anyone. After the ferry arrives in Paleochora and this story is solved and in the past, then ask me out for a coffee, okay?'

His eyes opened and he swallowed hard. 'Guess it is better than a no. Though, I had to say something. I hate being safe and quiet little Mark. You're incredible and you deserve to know that.'

Ioli smiled and raised her right hand to careless his unshaven cheek. 'You're a sweet guy. You sure you want to get mixed up with me? I am not the young girl you once knew.'

'All the better. I can't wait to meet the new you.'

Ioli withdrew her hand and without another word, she turned and walked off. 'That's it?' Mark called out.

'Yep. For now, smooth talker,' she replied, turning round her head and flashing him a full toothed smile.

Mark stood motionless, his heart beat racing faster than a Ferrari on a closed circuit, watching her vanish into the darkness of the hall. He heard her light steps as she went down the steps and he exhaled deeply. 'Well played, little Mark. Well played,' he quietly pep-talked to his inner, insecure self while wiping the cold sweat from his forehead.

Chapter 12

My right foot sank into the mud, squelching as it went down. The wintry landscape of Gavdos unfolded before my sore eyes. A few dying bushes around me shook in the strong wind. Ahead of me, a naked, twisted tree at the end of the cliff; a little, black figure of a person sitting under it. Behind it, the dark Libyan sea ran and met the grey sky.

'We're going on a bear hunt, we're gonna catch a big one,' a girl's voice sung.

I'd recognized that voice anywhere.

'Gaby?' I shouted out.

'Come on, dad. Let's play,' she called back and went back to singing.

I quickened my pace and struggled through the mud to reach her. Out of breath, barefoot as I was, I ran to her. Her long, curly hair fell in front, covering her face. She wore her pink Snoopy pyjamas and her favorite matching slippers. Her hands were combing her doll. Blood dripped from her hands; the doll wore a wedding dress drenched in blood. My eyes focused on the cut open throat of the doll. Just then, the doll's eyes snapped opened. It was Cassandra.

'I died and you just talk and talk and taaaalk...' she screamed. I stepped back and fell into the mud, awakening safe and sound, back in bed. I sat up, exhaled deeply and wiped the cold sweat from my forehead.

I turned to my right to check if I had woken up Tracy only to notice the bed empty on her side.

'Tracy?' I called out in the direction of the bathroom door, though not expecting an answer as there was no light underlining the wooden door.

Could she be down at breakfast?

Outside, the black from the crying clouds sky made it hard to see what time of day it was. I clumsily searched for my cell phone amongst all the junk I had thrown on my bedside table. It lay surrounded by my wallet, my watch, my book, my belt and a bunch of paper notes from yesterday's interviews. Six o'clock sharp, it read. Too early for breakfast.

I jumped out of bed naked, having kicked off heavy sheets and a heavier quilt. Winter or summer, I always slept as my mama brought me into the world. Men's Health magazine was to blame. Ever since a twenty-two year old Costa read about how sleeping naked benefited your testicles and your health in general, I was sold on the idea of sleeping naked.

My black boxers climbed up my legs and I rushed to the wardrobe to get dressed. Buttoning up my white shirt, I exited the room into the dark hallway. No lights had been turned on. Darkness roamed the house; everyone was still asleep.

Tracy, where the hell are you?

The line between maintaining your cool and panicking is a blurry one. My heartbeat accelerated like a Bugatti, my forehead produced sweat faster than the clouds produced rain outside, yet my mind kept on repeating how silly I was to worry and that Tracy probably just could not sleep and was enjoying a nice, hot tea in the kitchen below. Psychologists call these thoughts defense mechanisms of the mind. My last wall of defense fell as I reached the dark and empty kitchen. In a house where one dead body followed another, my wife was missing.

If this was not a time to panic, when is it? Baby, where are you?

I ran back up the stairs and into my room. Tracy's phone sat on her bedside table. There went the idea of calling her. I picked up my phone and dialled Ioli's number. Five dial tones later, a grumpy, scruffy voice managed to say my name.

'Costa?'

'Ioli, get up and come to my room. Now. Alert, no one.'

'What's going on?'

'I can't find Tracy,' I said, worry coloring my voice, making it shake faster than a Latin dancer.

'What the...? I'm on my way.'

My bladder reminded me of my morning needs. I walked into the bathroom, loosened my trouser's top button and pulled out my aching for release little friend. My lower back was vibrating, causing little pains as I peed. As I exhaled in relief, my eye caught a glimpse of the mirror. I froze in terror. A paper note stared back at me, stuck to the glass surface.

Sorry for the drastic measures, but I cannot risk everything happening in vain. I mean your wife no harm. Stay out of my business and you will see Tracy again. Meddle and she is gone forever. Do not play with me, I'll be watching. Back off. Let us all leave the island and classify Irene's death as a suicide and Cassandra's as murder from Maria Marousaki.

Four minutes later, Ioli rushed into the room to find me in a pitiful state sitting on the floor with my head against the bed. Her hair was tangled up and her face puffed up from heavy sleeping. Her eyes still sore and red.

'Costa?' her voice full of concern. I passed her the note. She read it carefully and then knelt beside me.

'Keep in mind that Tracy's safe,' she said and hugged me.

My hand stroked her cheek. 'Thanks, but what do we do now?'

'We play it cool. Whoever asks we say Tracy is in bed sick. We appear to be up to nothing, let the killer think we agree with his plan and after breakfast we go looking for Tracy. It's a tiny island with less than fifty houses, she has to be somewhere. I doubt she is being kept here in the house, who would risk that?'

'Very discreetly, we should check the cellars and the attic to be on the safe side.'

'Of course, boss. And don't worry. We will find her,' she said, trying to persuade both of us.

'What's going on?' the voice from the door startled us. Anna, Ioli's mother, stood in the doorway wrapped in her purple, flowery gown, staring at us. Ioli took one look at the closed bathroom door and replied 'Nothing, mama. Tracy woke up sick. She's in the bathroom throwing up.'

'Oh, the poor thing. I'll make her some tea and bring it to her.'

'I'll come with you,' Ioli said. She left with her mother, making sure it was her that would bring up the hot beverage. As they departed, my head fell into my arms. Clichés ran through my mind.

If anything happened to Tracy... This is all my fault... How the hell did 'they' take her...

I could not lose Tracy. After the death of our only child, we went our own ways. Now, back together at last she was kidnapped from right next to me. I knew if anything happened to her, it would be the end of me. My mind travelled to the days after Gaby's funeral. Tracy had left me right after the burial. Alone, I drove up to the cemetery and sat for hours next to her tombstone. Sometimes, I did not leave even when night fell around us. I could not accept that she was gone.

One night, I threw a shovel in the back of my car and drove up the hill of graves, determined to take Gabriella back home with me. My baby girl belonged to me. She was a part of me and I could not let her go. She haunted my dreams, day and night; still does. As the sharp edge of the shovel dug into the muddy ground, I knew I needed help, I knew I had to get away. I fell back and cried, eventually falling asleep upon her grave. The sun's first rays sneaked up to my eyelids and awoke me. The happy surroundings of birds tweeting and flowers opening up to the sun were in full contrast with my darkened, aching soul. I said my goodbyes, threw the dirty shovel back into my car, drove to the police station down on Joralemon Street, quit my job, went home, packed my things and left for the airport. Days later, I began working for the Hellenic Police in Athens with frequent trips to the psychologists in the program. Years later, I had finally 'got my shit' together as Ioli so elegantly put it and now, this.

Self pity is a depthless hell, Papacosta! Get your sorry ass off the floor and get to work!

The morning's breakfast could have been a part of Dante's hellish world. I sat in a surreal world of croissants and forest fruit jams, surrounded by people in deep mourning over the death of their loved ones and there I was, cool on the outside, melting inside by boiling rage. One of these people knew where my Tracy was.

My fist and my gun could persuade them.

Kallisto, sat uncomfortably between George and Leonida. On any given day, she would have been pleased to have fitted into her black Versace dress and been dining in a mansion on a Greek island. Yet today, the gloom and death around her had succeeded in dampening even her otherwise bright spirits. Her out-going, loud bubbly personality had always been her defense mechanism in a world that scared her. A world full of violence, of hate, of war, of death.

'Where is your mind travelling to?' Leonida asked.

'Death scares me,' she plainly and honestly answered.

'Doesn't it scare us all?' George inquired, in a whisper.

'Do you believe in life after death, George?' Kallisto lowered her head and threw a sideways look at him.

'Well, I think I do. Or I want to. I was raised Orthodox like all of us and as Christians we have...'

'Well, I don't,' she interrupted him. 'I'm not an atheist or anything; I just cannot find a way to believe such a fairytale and knowing that one day, sooner or later, I will not be around, scares me. Me, Kallisto, everything I am, gone forever. Never to think again, to feel any sort of emotion again. Non-existence. The end,' she said, waving her hands.

I watched her and for a moment a slight line of a smile struggled to move upwards upon my rough, unshaven face. A thing that amazes me in life is how we store memories and how a person, a word, a situation could force your mind to replay moments of the past.

Watching and listening to Kallisto brought two memories to the surface. The first one, a fond one; my mother whose hands and arms moved uncontrollably when she spoke. If anyone ever pointed it out to her, her reply was always a proud 'we are Greek, is there any other way of speaking?'

The second one, one of the saddest moments after Gaby's death. After the funeral, Tracy's sister held Tracy in her arms, fondly stroking her hair, letting her sister's tears run freely. Tracy had just lost her only child. Her sister knew that all she could do is be there and listen. Tracy's words created a black hole in my soul that day.

'She's dead, my little girl is gone. Forever! Eight years old, for fuck sake. Never to go to high school, never to get her heart broken by her first love, never to pick up a sport or learn to play the piano, never to marry. She will never get to do anything again. And it's all Costa's fault. I told him to switch to a desk job, but no. He had to be a mighty New York detective and now, our daughter has been gunned down in the street like an animal.'

Words I will never forget.

Ioli came and sat next to me, her plate filled with toast soaked in honey, slices of cheese and turkey ham.

'Eat up,' she whispered, and placed the plate in front of me.

'I must look like a right state for Ioli Cara to share her food,' I managed to joke, though my face did not move any muscles to show a jovial mood.

'Share? That's your plate. I left mine by the breakfast buffet.'

Besides Anneta Zampetaki who remained in bed, everyone gathered around the long, wooden table for breakfast. All gloomy and with signs of spending a restless night. Besides a few good morning wishes and whispered conversations between friends and family, silence mostly occupied the room.

'How is your sister, Mr Zampetaki?' Melissa kindly asked Cosma, who sat quietly opposite her.

'She is doing fine. She is a fighter, that one...' he began to say, ducked down into his bowl of wheat cereal. He paused as he lifted his head and stared at Melissa, making her lower her eyes. 'Thanks for asking, my dear girl.'

'Is she fine?' Ioli whispered to Mark, who met her at the buffet. He did not miss the chance to sit next to her.

'Yes. Though without a scan, I cannot tell if everything is A-okay on the inside. Let's hope for the best and as soon as we leave the island, she needs to visit the hospital in Chania.'

The four bridesmaids entered the room together. The way they moved in a herd was quite comedic. I understood the whole *we are friends in a foreign land comforting each other in a difficult time* scenario, but this was getting ridiculous. They had held hands, stroked each other's hair and hugged ever since Cassandra's death. Maybe Tracy's disappearance was making me cold. Maybe.

Jason, having finally made his choice, smiled at Amanda and moved to sit next to her.

'Will you be taking testimonials from the remaining members of the group?' Cosma asked, being the first to speak loud enough to be heard by all. 'It is our last day on the island.'

It will be your last day forever if Tracy is not found you smug prick.

'No, no need to rush. We aren't going anywhere. Let people enjoy their breakfast,' I replied.

'Do you really believe the ferries will come tomorrow?' Amanda asked.

'Let's hope so, my dear. I need to bury my wife and child,' he bluntly replied and ducked back down into his plate. Gloom spread throughout the room once again, strangling down any emotions of joy born by the news of the ferry's arrival.

'Why is he spreading hope?' Ioli whispered in my ear. 'I spoke to HQ this morning and they said the restrictions will be lifted the day after tomorrow.'

'You spoke to HQ? Have they done background checks on everyone?'

'Nearly. It's taking time as some are not even in the Greek system. They did find out that the real aunt Myrrine died peacefully in her sleep in a nursing home in Florida a couple of years back. She had no children so they informed a distant cousin of hers, who, also, has since passed away. No one bothered to call Greece, so we all presumed her still alive.' She paused, looked around her, bit down on her cherry jam covered toast and continued 'Let's excuse ourselves and I'll tell you the rest in the library.'

At that moment, others began to leave the breakfast table. Gianni got up first, grunting something about his knees and how the weather affected them. Anna, polite and elegant as always, thanked Cosma for the meal and wished that the saints provide him with strength through these dark, unkind hours. Their departure signalled the *OK-we-can-go-now* feeling around the table and as uncle Thomas aided his wife up, Ioli and I left the room unnoticed.

With the heavy library door behind us, Ioli continued.

'Only Jason and Alexandra have criminal records. Jason for reckless driving. He was drunk and stoned, and drove into a neighbor's front lawn. Alexandra, listen to this, for stabbing her ex in the shoulder.'

'You don't say. Under what circumstances?'

'Domestic fight that escalated. She stated that after throwing a vase at his direction, he attacked her, threw her to the floor and tried to rape her. She admitted stabbing him with a kitchen knife in self-defense. She got six months community service.'

'Anything else suspicious or unusual with the background checks?'

'Not really. Pretty normal stuff, though not everyone has been checked yet. I found out something I did not know. I don't even know if he knows to be honest.'

'Who?'

'Leonida.'

'What about him?'

'He was adopted as a baby. The documents do not reveal who his birth parents are; just that it was an unmarried, underage girl that gave him up.'

'It's funny if you think that he resembles George and Homer. I would not think twice that they were not blood-related.'

'I know, right? Also, I found out that my uncle Thomas was not all so innocent in his youth. He owned a strip club!' she said with amazement, her eyes opening wide and her jaw dropping slightly. 'I regret not running background checks on my family sooner.'

'The deeper you dig, the deeper the shit you may found yourself in.'

'One of your grandma's famous sayings, again?' Ioli asked.

'Nope, this one's all mine.'

'Yeah, it sounded like you,' she said, mocking me; only to pause realizing my tension. 'We will find her, Costa.'

I leaned in, nearer to her and lowered my voice. 'With the storm outside, the short amount of time since her disappearance and the fact that everyone is counted for and in the house...'

'You believe she is locked up somewhere in the house?'

'Yes. Used as a last played threatening card to keep us off the case,' I said, clenching my fists. 'We were warned to stay off the case and that is what we will show. No more discussing the case with anyone. Casually, we are going to stroll through this palace and head down to the basement. Then, the attic. The rooms will follow and will be the most difficult to search.'

'Difficult or not, it will be done,' Ioli reassured me.

The lavish environment diminished quickly as we opened the burgundy door that led to the employees' quarters. Having first checked that no eyes were around to witness us, we crept past the staff's lounge area, sneaking past the two tall butlers that welcomed us on our first day here. They were young men from the island that only worked as butlers whenever the Zampetaki family was entertaining a significant amount of guests; the rest of the time they were fishermen and during the summer time, they acted as waiters at the island's one and only beach bar. We did not get to interview them; however, both had mentioned that they were together watching a movie when Cassandra encountered her killer. Through the half opened door, I saw them dig into a bag of chips and enjoy cans of coke, relaxed on the lounge's worn in sofa. The TV was re-winded to yesterday's game and the pair of youths sat back to kill another day of nothing to do.

At the end of the colorless corridor, an old brown door stood open, its mouth revealing narrow steps descending into darkness.

'If she was here, the door would have been locked,' I said disappointed, my hand grabbing my lowering head. I ran my thumb and index finger along my closed eyes and squeezed at the height of my Greek nose.

'Let's take a quick peek and be on our way then,' Ioli said, her hand searching the inside wall for a switch. With a minor crackle, the two hanging light bulbs came to life, revealing a dump, cold, dusty room filled with the family's forgotten belongings. The center of the room's belly lay empty while every other corner was stacked with coveted artefacts and furniture of another era.

'Tracy? Tracy?' I whispered as loudly as I could. Silence.

Ioli wandered around the room, checking for any possible doors. None.

We headed back to the stairs, noticing the least dusty boxes in the storage room. I opened one out of curiosity. High school books, paintings, posters of teen bands, animal ornaments. The cardboard box next to it with clean Barbie dolls, washed teddy bears, Lego bricks and all sorts of toys.

'Attic?' Ioli asked interrupting my daydream of Gaby playing with a variety of toys and games on the day after her birthday or after Christmas. Joyful times carved into memory; sometimes creating smiles, other times dampening the spirits.

The two butlers had not moved a muscle and paid no attention to us sneaking by. I closed the burgundy door behind as and with no one in sight strolled casually away from the door. Ioli remained, her eyes examining the walls.

'Enjoying the art?'

'Just checking there is no secret space.'

'Secret space?'

'Like a panic room or something of the sort. The walls seem real thick in this house. I noticed it in the library and dining room, too. Maybe, I am just being too analytical and paranoid.'

I did not reply. She had lost me in thought; until the voice behind me startled me. My skin jumped and it shivered my bones.

'Good morning, again,' Anna said, walking towards me. 'Tracy feeling better?' she asked as her husband Gianni stood by his daughter, staring at the wall she seemed preoccupied by.

'She's feeling better, but stayed in bed to relax, thank you,' I mumbled, trying to catch a breath of the heated, stale air that floated through the closed up house; the rain constantly plummeting, hitting against the windows, forcing them to remain shut.

'What else is going on? Really?' Gianni spoke softly to his daughter, while looking over his shoulder at his wife.

'Dad, nothing is wrong...'

'Lollipop, it's me you are talking to. I read you easier than I read the Sunday Sports News,' he replied, maintaining the same gentle tone of voice. His hand rose and caressed his daughter's hair. 'What is bothering you?'

Ioli leaned closer to him. 'Nothing is what it seems. We have our theories, but I cannot elaborate more. You just keep an eye out for mum and play it safe. Stay in numbers. Sit around with uncle Thomas and auntie Georgia. The storm will pass eventually.'

Gianni's caring eyes read his daughter for a moment. 'Are we in danger?'

'Daddy, there is nothing to worry about. Just stay together and don't mingle too much with people we just met,' she replied. 'And that is all am saying for now!' she raised her voice as he opened his mouth. 'Don't say another word and stop looking over at mum. She is stronger than you think and to be honest, it is you I am worried about. Doctors are always telling you to take it easy and mama told me how your blood results suck, so go relax, treat this like a holiday and enjoy a glass of red wine or two.'

'Well, well, well. Being told off by my child. How the table has turned. I must be getting old,' Gianni said and raised his hands, signalling another defeat in conversation with his strong-willed daughter.

'What are you two on about again?' Anna inquired.

'Nothing,' they both simultaneously replied to her; a response she often received from them over the last thirty years or so.

'Uh, hmm,' Anna replied, her eyes fixed on them both. She turned back to me and advised me to get some rest, too. 'You look pale as a woolly, winter sheep. Go rest by your beautiful wife.'

'Will do.' I forced a smile and waited for them to stroll off. With Gianni and Anna gone, my facial muscles obeyed my heart and the laws of gravity, and journeyed down my face.

'We shouldn't show that we are snooping around. Whoever is doing this has threatened Tracy. We should split up. You go for a walk by the bedrooms. Act like you are going to see Homer or Mark or whoever you bump into. Check which rooms are closed. I'll head up to the attic. Rendezvous in the library. Whoever gets there first, sits and reads a book, acting normally.'

Her hand gently touched mine and without commenting more, she walked off, down the quiet, dimly lit corridor and past the Hellenic statue of Apollo that made the hall look more like a museum than a home.

Reaching the top of the stairs, I nodded hello to Christina, who as always was rushing around, clumsily attending to her daily chores. The long hall stretched emptily, so I quickened my pace towards the wooden steps that led up to the attic. The crackling of my back joined in with the crackling of the wooden floor boards and as the stairway turned me left, I ran into a startled George and a surprised Leonida.

'Hello, Captain,' Leonida said in a high pitched voice, as he dusted his bottom.

Were they sitting here, guarding the door to Tracy? My thought triggered my hand to journey inside my jacket, nearing my gun.

I did not get a chance to ask what they were doing sitting there as George started to mumble.

'Wherever you sit in this place, gloomy faces surround you. Leonida does not do death well and I cannot stand the sobbing. Best place to sit and have a normal chat, you see.'

I did not reply. My hand had reached my gun. Both stood before me, blocking my way, towering over me from a higher step.

'Well, we will be on our way,' Leonida cheerfully said and with a mischievous smile, he speedily rushed down the stairs. An awkward, snake line smile graced George's well shaved, wrinkle free face as he, too, sprinted down the steps causing the wooden floorboards to creak and release faint clouds of dust.

I did not let my mind soak in the scene that just took place and proceeded to battle up the stairs with vibrating pain in my back, weakness in my knees and breakfast swirling around my anxious stomach.

The flight of stairs darkened as I reached the top. Just a small, sealed rectangular window provided a dim light from the dark sky outside. It seemed to have escaped the onslaught of rain, maybe covered by the tuile toit covered roof.

I grabbed the icy knob of the brown door. Closed, yet unlocked. It gave way with a cacophonous, strident squeak. Light fell in from ceiling windows, creating squares of light upon the dusty, wooden floor. The inside of the room, half of what I was expecting to see. The right side, stacked with suitcases and boxes while the left side had two long tables. One with dozens of snowballs the size of my hand; the Louvre, the Statue of Liberty, the Big Ben, the Parthenon all sealed behind thin glass, standing amongst fake snowflakes. The second table with four heavy books; I open them to discover each book contained an array of stamps from around the world. I wiped my dusty finger on my blue shirt and moved to the back of the room. Remembering Ioli's idea, I checked for hidden doors or cavities. None were to be found. My Tracy was still missing.

Ioli fared no better luck one floor below. All went around, seemingly with nothing to hide. Bedroom doors were left open, people came and went from their rooms to the kitchen, to the library for a book or to one of the two TV loungers. Folks just killing time. All with their phone in their hand, checking the weather reports or calling a loved one and describing their holiday from hell.

Only the last door to the right remained closed. Homer's.

Ioli prepared to knock. She hesitated upon hearing voices from inside the room. Glancing around to notice if she was on the recipient end of any stares and seeing that she was not, she decided to place her ear on the wooden door. She brushed her black hair back and leaned forward.

'I... I had no idea. I don't want anything. This is the last thing on my mind. Keep it,' Homer said. The pause between his sentence and who spoke next caused Ioli's pores to start producing cold, winter sweat.

'To be honest, my dear lad, what the hell am I going to do with it?' Cosmas said. His voice weak, crackling, unsteady in tone.

Another long paused followed. Slight weeping echoed through the room. Ioli's brain painted the image of the two men holding each other, comforting one another in an unspeakable moment of anguish, despair and torment.

Footsteps coming towards the door brought her back from her thinking place. What money were the two men referring to? She jumped back a step or two and acted as if she had just arrived at the door as it flung open and Cosmas exited, nearly bumping into her.

'Oh, sorry. I was just coming to check in with Homer,' she apologized.

'You're a sweetheart,' Cosmas said, his eyes red and puffy. He placed his hand upon her shoulder and smiled a pitiful smile. 'Good luck with cheering him up. He is still young, joy can still be regained,' he said and ambled away.

Ioli took a deep breath and popped her head through the open door. Homer stood by the window, his gaze fixed on the rattan, garden chairs floating in the wavy, swimming pool waters. The pool had turned brown from the dirt and flowers it had gathered. The winds whistled through, calmer than before, yet still strong. The rain remained.

'Two days without a break. I hope it's not another thirty-eight to go,' Homer commented on the thick rain drops.

'Maybe we should build an ark and get the hell off this island.'

'Oh, Ioli. It's you,' Homer said, turning around quickly.

'Expecting someone else?' Ioli was fast to ask. Her head tilting to the side, she was studying Homer.

'Erm, no. Not really. Well, I thought it was Alexandra. She passed by before, saw Cosma here and left without interrupting.'

'Cassandra's girlfriends checking up on you?'

'Something like that.'

His tone of apathy irritated Ioli, but she was good at not showing her emotions. They always remained below the skin until she wished them to be revealed.

'Cosma looks ready to break down,' she changed the subject, mentally noting down to speak with Alexandra.

'I am ready to break down and his loss is double than mine.'

Ioli nodded her head in agreement and sat on the bed. She patted it with her right hand, urging Homer to sit beside her. Homer reluctantly approached. His manner resembled that of a school boy ready to be told off.

'How long were you outside the door?' he asked, sitting next to her.

'Long enough to overhear that money is about to come find you. A large amount of money, I presume.'

'Indeed,' Homer said. 'But I don't want it. It does not seem right, you know?' he was quick to add.

'Cassandra put you in her will?'

'I had no idea. When we got engaged, she admitted to me that her family was wealthier than what she had previously said. Especially her mother, she had stressed. Apparently, Cassandra had a will drafted just a few days ago, leaving all her belongings to any future children. But until then, she filled me in as her heir.'

'And did she have a lot in her name?'

'That is what Cosmas just found out from his lawyers. His wife had transferred all her money to Cassandra, a few months ago. Probably shortly after hearing about the wedding.'

'How much money, if I may ask?'

'Near 800,000 Euros.'

Ioli whistled upon hearing the number. 'That's a lot of money.'

'I know. And now I am torn...'

'Torn? Why?'

'I would never accept any house or land that was in her mother's family for centuries when I was a part of the family for like five seconds, but money is money. It seems so wrong to accept it, but then again if I give it to Cosmas, who will inherit it? His sister?'

'Or a charity.'

'I thought about that myself. Give a percentage to charities that fight for children. Cassandra would have loved that.'

'A percentage?'

'Oh, come on, Ioli. Don't be so condescending.'

'I'm not. I am just so used to murders happening, and they always happen for love or money or both.'

Homer stood up. Fury flashed across his eyes. He clenched his fists as his face turned a faint shade of red. In the cold room, his armpits had managed to form two little dark lakes on his blue shirt.

'Are you accusing me of murdering Cassandra for money? I told you, I just found out. I had no idea about the money. I did not even know they were *this* rich.'

'I am not accusing you of anything, Homer and lower your tone of voice with me. I am simply pointing out how it will look, you keeping all that money and all.'

'Well, she left me the money and that is a fact I and everyone else will have to deal with. I could not care less how the gossiping old ladies and boring asses will take it. Let them talk.'

His voice came out strong and angry. Ioli stood up and approached him slowly. She rubbed his arm and laid a kiss on his unshaven cheek.

'Calm down. I am on your side.'

'I know,' he replied and took her into his arms. His jaw rested on her shoulder and there, Homer finally shed his gathered tears.

Minutes later, Ioli left the room confused. It sure did not look good that he would come into so much money and for some reason, Alexandra visiting him did not sit well with either of her inner instincts, woman's and detective's. She had lied about being on his side. Ioli was on one side and one side only. The truth's. And with that in mind, she set off to find Alexandra.

I kept to our plan and made my way to the library.

The door stood closed. The door knob warmed my hand as I grabbed it. The fire inside burnt hot. I entered the room and closed the door behind me. Dozens of oak logs were wrapped in flames in the majestic, marble fireplace. The flames reached high, disappearing into the dark cavity that vacuumed the grey smoke and released it into the cold, rainy outside. The room's high temperature forced me to immediately remove my beige jacket. My body was never fond of high temperatures. My armpits were always begging to return to New York and its one month of summer.

'Too hot for you, Captain?' a shaky voice asked.

I did not need to turn to recognize that tone. 'Mrs Helena, I did not see you there.'

'You young ones have warm blood running around your veins. My relic of a body needs a good fire on days like these. I guess, I will have the girls light me a bonfire if this maddening, nuisance storm from hell continues.'

I smiled and walked nearer to where she was sitting. She had pushed one of the tall armchairs back to the wall, placing it right between the two towering bookcases. The thin, green book in her slightly trembling hands caught my attention.

'Peter's long walk by Alki Zei? That brings back memories,' I said.

'And what memories are those?'

'Greek high school back in Astoria. We read the book as part of a school project. It was the only book the school made us read that I loved. A simple story with such powerful lessons. The first book that really got me thinking,' I admitted. I paused, realizing that it was my first seconds of not thinking of Tracy. A weird sensation of guilt came over me. Tracy was God-knows where and I stood nice and warm in a library discussing childhood books.

'I see. Pleasant memories. Yes, it is a powerful book. However, my memories are quite different.'

More guilt. The old lady was probably a child during World War II just like Peter.

'I was nine years old when the Nazis took Athens and hunger spread throughout the land. My mother worked as a dressmaker in a little shop down by the docks. We witnessed hundreds of young men, most not even with a mustache yet, gather on old, rusty boats and head off to the mainland to fight for mama-Greece. Nearly none returned,' she continued.

I sat down in the armchair behind me and remained quiet. Never interrupt an old lady retelling the past. Helena Zampetaki's eyes grew watery.

'I remember the day my father left, like it was yesterday. I might not be able to remember what I ate for breakfast, yet I'll never forget that day. The air was chilly and we said our goodbyes inside the shop. My parents kissed and hugged, my mother standing strong for my sake. I remember my father kneeling before me, tears in his eyes. I had never seen him cry before that day. *My sweet baby girl*, he whispered and sucked me into his huge arms. I screamed as he let go and walked out the door, never to be seen again.'

'That's terrible, I...'

'No need for sympathy, Captain. To lose a parent is much more natural than to bury a child.'

'How did...'

'I know more than what people believe I do.'

I stood up and approached her, kneeling in front of her. 'And what do you know more about Cassandra's and Irene's death?'

'Nothing, of course,' she said out loud. However, she placed her index finger upon her thin lips while with her other hand, she invited me closer. As my head reached near her lips, she whispered to me. My eyes opened wide upon hearing her words.

Meanwhile, as truths came to life in the library, Ioli made her way to find Alexandra.

As expected, Cassandra's four bridesmaids were together. Dressed in black, they clashed with the bright and colorful background of the TV lounge downstairs. The television was playing on mute; Amanda sat opposite it, staring at the moving images with sleep craving eyes. Next to her, Jenny managed to balance her o'verweight by any standards' body and lay spread out on the multicolored sofa. Andrea stroked her dyed blonde hair by the ten foot tall oval window. Her gaze noticed everything and nothing. The rain fell, the earth welcomed it and trees fought to stay up straight. Just like the day before.

The person of interest sat in a tall back armchair by the fireplace. The fire had died down, a few sparks crackled among the thin logs of wood and flames came to life, only to fade back down into the pine tree wood. Alexandra had tied her brown hair up into a knot, held only by her bitten pencil. Her legs rested on a round, three-legged wooden stool and her hands held up a Madame Figaro magazine to eye level. She did not notice Ioli enter the room and beeline towards her. Ioli focused on Alexandra's eyes as they travelled around, scanning the magazine. She flicked through the pages nervously, each page producing a sharp noise as it was forced to give way to the next.

'Nothing of interest to read?' Ioli asked.

Alexandra lowered the magazine and sat up straight, retrieving her long legs from the stool. 'I did not notice you there. Ioli, right?'

Ioli nodded. 'Can we speak in private?'

Alexandra's face darkened for a second. A shadow of doubt rolled across her face, but with a bright, wide smile Alexandra replied 'I guess I never did get a chance to give a statement, what with the power going out and that woman falling down the stairs.'

Ioli walked ahead, her eyes slipped into their corners making sure Alexandra followed her. She did, somewhat reluctantly and with her friends' eyes focused on her. Ioli noticed that none of her girlfriends asked why she was being summoned alone. No whispery *what's going on* or silent mouth movements or hand gestures. Ioli could not shake the shivers that her inner instinct sent to her.

Ioli looked up and down the long corridor and leaned on the cherry red wall. Alexandra dragged her silky hair to one side and stopped a foot away from Ioli.

'On the night of Cassandra's death, I was with the girls. We share a joined two bedroom...'

'That is not what I want to know.'

Alexandra straightened her body and squinted her hazelnut eyes.

'I thought that you were supposed to note down our whereabouts at the time...'

'Why do you keep going up and checking on Homer?' Ioli asked, sure that she had visited him before.

Alexandra stood before her, lost for words. She stumbled on a few vowels before forming a sentence. 'He... Homer... was... err... Cassandra, my friend... erm... her fiancé and now she is dead, I wanted to make sure he was alright. I owe it to Cassie.'

'Say his name again.'

'What?'

'His name.'

'Homer?'

'Hmm.'

'OK, this is getting ridiculous. What is it...'

'Lower your voice. I'm still in a good mood. You don't want to change that. Besides, you don't want everyone hearing that you and *Homer* were, let's say, *close*.'

'I don't like what you are implying.'

'I could not care less about what you like or not. And I am not implying anything. I am simply stating a fact.'

'Who told you? Is Amanda talking shit again?'

Ioli had her answer, her proof. Disappointment fell down hard. Her sweet cousin Homer, all of a sudden was being portrayed in her mind as a cheating bastard and a gold digger.

'Did Cassandra know?'

Alexandra's fingers rubbed her sweaty palms. She looked flushed and spoke with difficulty. 'I know how things must sound. I have judged friends like this many times before, but as bad as it sounds, I never intended it to happen. Neither did Homer. He loved Cassie. I loved her, too.'

'That's a lot of love to handle.'

'Be as sarcastic as you wish. It all started two years ago, after Homer and Cassie had a big argument and he stormed out of their apartment.'

'What did they fight about?'

'Money was always an issue with those two. Both were deep in student debt and both ambitious to keep studying and earning more certificates. Anyway, Homer and my brother were close and he crashed at my brother's apartment for a few days. I stayed there, too. Well, I see no reason to spell things out for you. The all time classic tale, about one thing leading to another. It was just for fun. We never fell for each other. During the last two years we probably only slept together a handful of times.'

'Only, huh?'

'Look, I have no reason to stand here, being belittled by you. Our affair, if it can be called that, has nothing to do with Cassie's death...'

'That's my job to decide.'

Alexandra exhaled deeply, her watery eyes trembled and she leaned back onto the flowery wall. 'She was murdered by that crazy old lady.' The sentence sounded more like a question.

'Don't know about crazy, but hell yeah, she was old. Maybe too old to stab with such force a strong, young woman like Cassandra. Maybe, she had help. Maybe a bitch in heat looking to gain the lover she denies falling for.'

Alexandra broke away from the wall and raised her right hand.

'Oh, please. I am looking for an excuse to channel my anger, right now,' Ioli calmly said, remaining still as a Greek statue.

Alexandra grunted, lowered her shaking arm and stormed off back to her friends. Ioli watched her disappear through the doorway, fixed her hair and turned to come find me in the library.

Ioli entered the room, just as grandma Zampetaki sauntered out. Ioli greeted her, only to receive a grunt of a reply from Mrs Helena who did not bother to stop or look at her.

'Charming old woman, isn't she?' Ioli asked, pushing the door behind her. I remained still where I stood, in the center of the room with my back to the imposing, cherry wood bookcase.

'You will never believe what I just found out. Homer...' Ioli began to say. She paused upon witnessing my index finger slowly reach my lips and signal her to be quiet. My eyes begged her to change the topic.

'... supports Olympiakos, can you believe it? As a kid, he was a great Paok fan,' she continued.

Clever girl.

'And you think you know certain people.'

'You can say that again, boss.'

I walked towards her and my lips formed the words *follow me*. 'I better be heading up to check if Tracy's flu is still tormenting her.'

'Give her my love. Have you seen my parents, by any chance?'

'I think they are in the dining room hall with your uncle and aunt.'

'That's where my next stop will be then.'

Industry expects and movie fans would have called our acting wooden, but we put on a show nevertheless.

Chapter 13

Athens, years ago

'I love you!' Achilles shouted, as he jumped up and down opposite Agatha.

Sweaty backs formed their surrounding environment; an environment of loud music, flashing lights and the sharp smell of alcohol. Mercedes Club always let in an illegal -based on their space- number of clubbers. Athens youth filled the dance floor, none the less. Exam results came back and good or bad, the end of the semester was reason for celebrating.

Agatha had more reason than others. Ten out of ten in all subjects. First of her year. She dyed her hair red -another teen dream of hers- and wore her brand new blue dress which revealed her deep cleavage and showed more than enough leg. She noticed Achilles' lips move and paused. Did he really say what she thought he did?

'What?' she yelled back, bringing an ecstatic Achilles to a halt.

He leaned forward, bringing his face opposite hers. He wiped his sweaty palms on his jeans and placed them on her cheeks, pulling her close; their lips inches from each other. He stared into her eyes for what seemed like minutes to Agatha, yet the same Madonna song still played. The kiss that followed weakened her knees and provided security of her belief of what he said. Achilles pulled back, gently biting her bottom lip, taking it with him. He let go and screamed 'I said, I love you!'

A few girls dancing next to them turned around and giggled until common jealously kicked in.

'I love you, too, you silly, crazy, sexy beast you!' Agatha replied and leapt into his arms.

Two hours and a dozen kisses later, the couple and another twenty late-nighters vacated the club. The lights had been switched on and two songs later, the music had stopped.

'Where to now?' Achilles said and chuckled drunkenly.

'Do you know what time it is?' Agatha asked. 'The sun will be up, soon.'

'My point exactly. It's so late, it's early.' His silly grin never leaving his sweaty face.

'What do you have in mind?' Agatha inquired, lowering her voice and adding a sexy tone.

'My place... or yours,' Achilles finally said the words he had always wanted to say. They had been dating for months and Agatha had never once invited him to her apartment, neither had she come to his. She always had an excuse ready and they always met in public. Achilles eagerly waited for a reply. He could not stand to be tormented by his friends, again.

'In a meaningful relationship, sex isn't *that* important,' he tried to defend himself to his mates.

'Yeah, unless you aren't getting any,' Pavlo joked.

'Agatha's a good girl. She is not like the sluts you horny dogs chase after,' he retaliated.

'Yes, that is why we have doggy style, rough sex and you are still waiting to have Amish style sex with Miss Goodie!' Mario said, and laughed out loud.

The meaningful conversations among eighteen year olds never change.

'Did you hear me?' Agatha asked again.

'Huh?'

'I said my place.'

Achilles' eyes widened as much as they could. He jumped off the pavement, landing in a drain pipe puddle, waving his hands to stop the approaching cab. The taxi driver slammed down on the brakes. The tires screeched on the wet asphalt road and a cloud of smoke from his exhaust flew forward and surrounded the young couple. The driver shook his clean shaven head and murmured something about crazy, youthful love. He had seen his fair share of couples exiting the notorious night club over the years; some remained the same, some changed partners more often than he changed socks. He listened to the directions from the sweet girl and winked at the boy. The gear got pushed into place and the vehicle set off for its short-lived journey. The driver drove in silence; only the sound of kissing being heard. He discreetly gazed upon the young couple, especially when Achilles' right hand journeyed up Agatha's firm leg.

Ten minutes later, the driver received a generous tip and watched the crazy, young ones run to the building's door. Watching them, he pulled out his phone and sent his wife a text. *Love you sleepy head, just like when we were young*, he typed, making a few typos with his fat fingers along the way. In a few hours, he would provide a broad smile to his wife's face. A king's breakfast and morning cuddles waited for him when he arrived home from a long nine hour shift. A successful marriage is all about the details. The small gestures that let you know your other half still cares.

Upstairs, Agatha, pleased with having cleaned and tidied her apartment just the previous day, lit her bedroom's vanilla-scented candles and turned on the air-con. Nothing worse to kill the mood than more sweat. Her eyes observed Achilles undress down to his navy blue boxers; his huge front bulge catching her eye. She had never seen a naked man before. Shivering in the excitement, she unzipped her dress and let it fall to the floor. Achilles bulge shook before her. He approached her and pulled her into his arms. His hands ran freely down her back, while his tongue explored her ear lobes and her neck. She pushed Achilles onto the bed and fell on top of his shaped abs and his chiselled chest. His fingers slowly pulled down her pink panties and then, slid up and fiddled with her bra. Soon, she sat naked upon him. Taking a deep breath, she found the courage to undress him. She found it funny how his penis jumped out and wiggled before her, yet showed no such emotion. Nervously, she bowed down and let her tongue journey along his hard erection. He leaned back in euphoria. She continued upwards, longing to reach his lips. They kissed with force and Achilles swirled them around with adroitness, finding his way on top of her and finally, in her. Wet as she was, he entered her with ease and did not take his time, pushing himself in. Agatha gasped in pain. Achilles immediately pulled out.

'I'm sorry. I...'

'Sssh,' she said, placing her finger upon his lips. 'Take it, slowly. It is my first time, you know.'

Moments later, she could not believe her new outgoing personality when she whispered 'not, *that* slow.'

The whole six minutes seemed like an hour to burning-up Agatha. Achilles pulled out and came on her lower belly. She stared in amazement; her curious nature enjoying something new.

Huffing and puffing, Achilles fell to her side. His hand lay upon her breast; her beating heart forcing it to bounce. His lips met hers and his eyes relaxed, gently staring into hers.

'Told you, I love you. I'm so glad you let me show you how much.'

'You're the best thing that has ever happened to me,' she replied breathlessly.

Words she never forgot. Who could ever forget the words one regrets the most?

Chapter 14

The deserted laundry room rigged of flowery based detergent blended with dirty clothes. The maids had gathered all the guest's dirty laundry, yet had not turned any washing machines on. I bee-lined to the single window of the room, pulled back the cheap, thick, once-white curtains and despite the strong winds patrolling the house, I slid the glass window to the right. Ioli shivered as the icy wind danced around her, forcing her to close up her jacket buttons all the way to her chin. The sound of droplets crushing into muddy puddles echoed in the low-ceiling room.

'Costa, what's going on?'

'We are being fools, that's what!'

Under any other circumstances, she would have retaliated at the insult. Now, she approached me and laid her hand upon my shaking shoulder. My nerves were getting the best of me.

'Calm down. Tell me what it is you have figured out.'

'Figured out? Nothing! Told, yes. We were being watched in the library. With a mansion like this, we should have known better.'

Ioli stepped back and tilted her head to the side. 'Cameras?'

'Bingo. And not only in the library. The old lady said her daughter-in-law was obsessed with security and had them installed everywhere. 'Gossiping tart', she called her, always listening in on everybody's conversations. That is why the old lady sat in spots that were blind to the cameras.'

Ioli's eyes widened. 'And why Katerina kept looking up when we interviewed the maids. The way she stared at Christina badmouthing her boss...'

'And why the maids and butlers come here to talk. No cameras down here or in the bedrooms, the old lady said.'

Ioli exhaled with a sigh. 'That is how our suspect knew we were on to them.'

'That is why they took Tracy. God, we were so stupid. We should have known and we would have been more careful and I would have kept closer to Tracy and...'

'Costa, this is not on you. And we will find her. I swear.'

'The thing is we don't know who to trust. Watching the surveillance tapes could crack our case. But, with Tracy being held...'

I fell back onto the wooden bench against the moldy wall. My hands rubbed my eyes for a few seconds and ran through my messy hair. 'What is it that I would not believe about Homer? Besides his football team preference?'

It was Ioli's turn to sit down and fall back against the aging wall.

'Though he denies knowing anything about it, apparently Cassandra had tons of cash in her name, inheritance from her mother. Guess who receives it?'

It was my hand's turn to touch her shoulder. Homer had fallen off the pedestal.

'Wait, it gets better. For the last two years or so, he has been having an on-off affair with Alexandra.'

'Did Cassandra know?'

'That is something I have to grill Homer about. Alexandra admitted no such thing.'

'Ioli, if Homer knew about the cameras and how to access them...'

'I know. That is what has been on my mind. I keep replaying his words in my head. He did say that Cassandra gave him the grand tour of the place.'

'Cosmas knows for sure. So does Katerina and grandma Zampetaki.'

'Anneta could know, too. She seems really close to her brother.'

'Whoever heard us talk about the case, must have gotten scared that we knew Irene's death was not a suicide and how we suspected the old lady had an accomplice and panicked. Panicked enough to kidnap Tracy. Ioli, we have to find her.'

'You checked the attic, right?'

I nodded. My eyes revealing processes at work. Ioli could read me like an open book.

'What's bothering you?'

'Sexual orientation.'

'Come again? You lost me.'

'Never mind, for the time being. It will be my last card. I want to go outside and look for Tracy. They could not have taken her very far. I will explore the gardens. If I come back empty handed, then I will throw down my last playing card. Work on any suspicion, trust your gut,' I finished with Ioli's trademark advice to rookie cops.

'There's a lot of I's in your sentence. I'm coming with you,' she said and stood up.

'The world is coming to an end outside...'

'And I look like cheap silicone to you? Besides, if anything happens to you, who would know where the heck you are? Zip it, I'm coming, end of discussion,' she said, ordering my mouth to retreat. I raised my hands in defeat.

We both stood by the window, silently witnessing the downpour. Thunder and garden items rolling around broke the sound of constant rain. I closed my eyes. Tracy's wide smile came to mind. Determined as a wounded, raging bull, I lifted myself up and leapt out the window. I stood by the safety of the house's wall, while Ioli came out after me.

'Let's make a dash for the pool house. The killer might have figured no one would approach with Cassandra's body being there.'

'No,' I replied. 'You go. I'll head out to that abandoned shed over there,' I said, pointing to the relic of a cottage by the old, stone wall that surrounded the mansion's land. 'No need for you to risk coming out there.'

I think Ioli was too cold to argue. She nudged me on my right shoulder, tied her hair into a tight bun and looked around, focusing on the windows of the house. No peeping eyes gave the signal to run out into the storm. I watched as she nearly lost her balance on the wet tiles by the wavy swimming pool and tripped over a rolling ceramic flower pot by the door of the pool house. She paused, signalled me a thumbs up and took out her gun.

By the time she entered, I had run along the mansion's side wall, cursing at my weak knees and ever-growing stomach pains. I stopped at the end of the house -the last point of safety- and gazed out into the hostile surroundings of muddy fields that lead up to the crumbling down in the rain cottage with the broken door and the smashed in window.

Step by step, I fought an uneven battle with nature's forces. My feet sank deep into the mud, making every next step heavier and harder to take. Tracy's image, imprinted in my mind, gave me strength to follow.

The wind pushed hard against my body, my thin hair blew around and my eyes were forced to shut. Determined, I reached the crumbling cottage and kicked in the broken door. The smell of rodents and feces blended with the clean, fresh air blowing in through cracks in the wall. The wind was howling as the rats ran and scattered back into dark corners. The room was deserted.

'Tracy,' I yelled out, more out of anger than a cry for an answer.

Ioli had no better luck. Out of fear of being watched by a hidden security camera, she acted as if she had gone to see the body and while there, strolled casually into the kitchen in search for a drink. The entire time, her eyes were searching around and her ears were alert for any cries for help. It was just her and the body.

Defeated, we both returned to the house, unsure of our next steps.

Chapter 15

Athens, years ago

It was the first day of August and the third day of the menacing heat wave; a perfect day for island getaways. The port of Piraeus welcomed into its deep blue stomach everything ranging from the world's largest cruise ships to ten-sitter ferries. The sizzling, Greek sun attacking the skin of people walking under it and illuminating all that stood below it. Hats, sunscreen, umbrellas, cold water; all were unable to save you from the heat and the sweat. Nevertheless, smiles were shining all around and holiday makers glowed with delight and a carefree mood.

Achilles carried Agatha's luggage upon the ferry that playfully bounced on the deep, blue waters. She followed in a short, yellow dress and a hat she referred to as glamorous. It was her first holiday with her first boyfriend. Achilles planned everything for their getaway to the majestic island of Naxos.

They were going to walk hand-in-hand through a web of steep cobbled alleys in the main town of Hora, shop from the many traditional shops and visit beautiful old churches, the ancient ruins of Apollo's and Dionyso's temples and several Venetian castles, all coexisting in harmony with the Cycladic cubic houses perched high along the green hills that overlooked the fertile valleys and lush green gorges. They would visit isolated, atmospheric beaches and of course, try kite boarding.

Agatha day-dreamed of the magic awaiting her. Romantic meals by the harbor, clubbing at night and making love to Achilles. She planned on giving Ariadne and Dionysos, the two famous lovers of mythology, a run for their money.

Soon, the largest island of the Cyclades came into view, surrounded by the ocean.

Agatha giggled as she hugged Achilles from behind.

'Thank you,' she whispered into his ear, biting gently on his earlobe.

The ship settled into the calm waters of the picturesque harbor and Agatha and Achilles were the first to disembark. Full of joy they rushed to the rental office, situated between an ice-cream parlor and a souvenir shop. Achilles had already booked them a car. They were going to stay at his relatives' cabin.

'Bit out of town, isn't it?' Agatha asked after the first ten minutes of driving through empty-of-buildings fields.

'Yes,' Achilles answered with a shaking voice. 'If I remember well, there's a beach within walking distance. Kind of rough compared to the ones near town, but we have the car so don't worry. We will be eating out and clubbing and drinking at the cosmopolitan beaches all day.'

Agatha placed her hand upon his and gently caressed it. She never understood why she loved the rough, brutal feel of it. Its hairy, scratchy surface was just like her father's. Maybe psychologists were right; maybe all girls had an Electra complex.

The scenery unravelled from the car's open window. Weather defying olive trees stood majestically in the dried, summer land that journeyed to the tranquil sea. The ocean breeze with its distinct freshness and smell of salt filled the moving car.

'There it is,' Achilles announced interrupting her day-dreams.

Agatha's gaze travelled to the humble, wooden cabin built in the middle of a vine leaf field. It looked outdated; its paint scratched, the wood splinted by the ever-burning Greek sun and the windows with the tinted glass were dusty. The hanging porch light, tarnished over the years, swung and creaked in the smooth, summer breeze with the salty, sea fragrance.

Achilles steered the car down the dirt road that cut through the wild grass and led to the two bedroom house. A large cloud of dirt grew behind them and attacked the house as Achilles slammed on the brakes and parked the vehicle right next to the aging porch.

Agatha waited before stepping out, giving the dust time to settle. She wondered how much time she would need to get settled.

'*If only men could accept a woman to pay for a decent hotel in town*,' she thought and took the plunge into the wild, Greek countryside. The porch steps creaked and groaned as her light foot made contact.

Achilles rushed by her, key in hand and with effort he unlocked the door.

'This way,' he smiled awkwardly.

Inside, the air lingered thick and stale. A layer of dust covered the kitchen counters, the table and chairs and the twenty year old TV. Agatha stood unsure. Two open doors revealed a bedroom and a bathroom even in worse off states. House chores were definitely not on her holiday menu.

'Great isn't it?' Achilles asked. His dumb question pulling Agatha's last straw.

'Are you freaking kidding me? Can you see how dirty everything is? And where are we supposed to sleep? We did not bring sheets and I am definitely not sleeping on that old rusty piece of shit. Can't you see how dirty the bed is? Rats have shit all over it!' Agatha's rant began; her voice rising with each word. Achilles' face turned cold as if the spark in his eyes was suddenly switched off. It was almost as if he had turned into another person before her eyes; a completed stranger.

'Well, you know what your royal highness? You aren't sleeping in the bed,' he snapped and grabbed her by the hair, pulling her with his fists clenched inside her flock of gold hair. Agatha yelled; in pain, in shock? She could not tell. 'Revenge time, you ugly bitch,' he coldly said and forcefully punched her in the face. Agatha fell to the ground. With eyes half opened, she noticed Achilles pull back the rugged carpet and lift up a hatch. A secret cellar was built under the cabin. With a kick to her side, Achilles rolled her body into the open cavity. She cried out as her rib snapped on the first step down. Her hands searched for something to hold on to, but nothing was to be found. She rolled down the flight of twelve steps before crashing into the cement ground below.

'Welcome to hell, whore!' Achilles called out and slammed down the hatchet's wooden door. Agatha sat up in pain; trembling in complete darkness.

Chapter 16

The ferocious winds patrolling the hill that housed the Zampetaki mansion had eventually calmed down –not in your everyday ocean breeze way, yet calmer than the near-hurricane winds of the previous days. The rain fell in the same quantity as before, showing no sign of withdrawing. It fell straight down to earth; the big drops of water not bothered by the winds any more. Drops fell into the pool, into muddy puddles, into streaks of water. Water travelled around the house, down to the pool house and over the cliff, leaping down to the newly formed river. Water journeyed by the old shed at the end of the estate and gathered behind it, plunging through the gaps of the iron bars that were placed to protect the children of the Zampetaki family from plummeting down into the old, deep, sealed-off sewage hole. A small scale stream dropped ten or so feet and began filling up the once cavernous hole. Most of the space had been filled in with dirt when the house boasted a new, updated sewage system and the old tunnels were deemed unnecessary.

It was in this confined space where Tracy awoke. She woke as if waking up after a painful procedure at the hospital. She felt all the symptoms described by her mother after having her appendix removed. Drowsiness and numbness held her down, half-sunk into the mud below. The watery earth rising by the second had reached her opened mouth. Tracy struggled to sit up, her head wobbling side to side. Her eyelids rose slowly, revealing her underground prison. Tracy screamed, yet felt sure that she did not produce a loud enough sound. She could not gather enough strength to stand up. Her mind was playing fragmented images from the night before.

Her bladder had been growing inside her, asked to be relieved. She sneaked out of bed and without turning on the lights, she headed to the bathroom. As she exited the bathroom, she gasped at the sight of the bedroom's open door. She turned to see her heavy sleeper of a husband had not moved a single muscle. Uncertain, she tiptoed to the open door, peeped through it. No one was there. She opened the door a few more inches and stepped a foot out into the dark hallway. Suddenly, a wet cloth covered her mouth and nose; an awful smell of medicine; her head smacked against the wall. These were her last memories before opening her eyes in what she presumed to be a well.

With her head heavy and leaning back, she brought her right wrist up to eye level.

'Shit,' she breathlessly cursed. Her watch had vanished from her hand. She had no clue how long she had been down that hell hole. She didn't guess she had been out for a whole day; although weak, light managed to sneak in through the iron bars.

Her mind travelled to her detective husband.

'Had he not noticed me missing? He and Ioli must be searching for me...'

Blood running through her once numb legs made her feel stronger. With trembling hands upon the muddy walls, she struggled to stand up. Her feet sank deeper into the muddy floor. A steady flow of water fell beside her. Her eyes focused on a wild, miniature, purple flower growing out of the wall. It hung, half dipped in muddy water, half in the icy air. The water gradually swallowed its bottom leaf.

'Oh, my god. The water is rising,' Tracy said, her voice strained, shaky and tired.

She swung around 360 degrees. Around her only clay walls, below her the rising sludge and above her a circle of crepuscular light, obstructed by four rows of iron bar. She was trapped.

More awake now, she screamed at the top of her lungs. Again and again. There was no reply. She stopped, panting, with tears gathering at the corner of her eyes. Outside, loud thunder mocked her pitiful attempts at being heard.

She wiped her forehead, noticing the blood for the first time. She followed the line of dried blood into her messed up, soaking wet, muddy hair, all the way to a round bump. She had cut open her head during her fall in the hallway. Or maybe when she was flung like a piece of trash down the hole. Her legs bore multiple scratches. Weirdly she felt no pain. Maybe the drug used to knock her out, numbed the pain. Maybe it was the shock.

That is when she realized how naked she was. Underwear and a ripped, once clean, once light blue gown were all she wore. The air around her was freezing. She shivered at the thought of being down there over night when temperatures were sure to fall. That is if the water did not consume her first.

'Oh, Costa, where the hell are you?'

She yelled again, her yells for help growing more hysterical with each call. She punched the wet walls and clumsily tried to climb up them. Each time falling back into the brown pool that had now reached her knees. Not knowing what else she could do, she leaned against the walls and cried. She closed her eyes and thought of her daughter. Her murdered angel. The thought of maybe meeting her, somehow being with her soon, soothed her.

Lightning illuminated her jail and two eyes staring through the iron bars frightened her.

'Who's there? Help me,' she screamed. The dark figure above did not reply, just retreated.

'Where are you going? You coward. Come back. Why are you doing this to me? I'll fucking kill you, you hear me. My husband will find me and he will find you, too. Aghhh!'

Her last scream joined the thunder.

She felt helpless. In her dismay, Tracy sat down and did the only thing she could.

Wait.

Chapter 17

*The chapter contains a graphic rape scene. If you do not wish
to read the scene, skip to the end of the chapter.*

Time diminishes in the darkness. We are left alone with all our
fears and wait for our survival instincts to surface.

Left alone for hours, Agatha cried, sitting on the cool cement
floor before an inner pep talk to get a hold of herself. She stood up
and staggered around the dark room, hands stretched out in front of
her, waving them around in the blackness. She soon reached the
prickly, cement wall and with shaking hands she searched. A switch
for a light, a door, a window; anything. Having reached the corner,
she continued on. Her leg hit upon something metallic. She leaned
forward and let her hands explore. Soft. It was a bed. She shivered at
her first wild thoughts.

*Is someone staying down here? What if I am not alone? Is this
bed for me? Am I going to be kept a prisoner for long?*

And the question that was on her mind since her fall down the
stairs: *Why is Achilles doing this to me?*

Agatha swept away her tears from the corners of her eyes and
continued on, around the bed and back to the cold wall. Soon, she
reached the stairs. Down on all fours, she struggled with her broken
rib to reach the top. She banged manically on the cellar's door,
screaming at the top of lungs to be let out. She begged Achilles to be
reasonable; she yelled 'I love you'.

Only then did she receive any sort of response. Laughter. Wicked laughter. Heavy laughter by multiple men. Her eyes widened in horror.

Who is up there? What the hell is going on?

On the floor above, Achilles' father finished off his whiskey and slammed down the cheap glass.

'OK, boys. That's enough drinking. Time to play,' he said, a wicked, mischievous grin forming across his sunburnt face.

His brother, Valentino, hugged him from behind and kissed his cheek. 'Revenge!'

Valentino's two sons stood up simultaneously from the filthy sofa. The coffee table in front of them was filled with empty beer bottles.

Achilles knelt down by the hatchet's wooden lid and yelled. 'Get your ass back down, right now or I will kick you down there, again.' He placed his ear upon the door and listened as Agatha struggled to turn around and crawl back down. He, then, pulled the door open, while his uncle Valentino switched on the lights from the kitchen above.

Two hanging light bulbs flicked to life and burned Agatha's eyes. Her sight blurry; she thought she saw shadowy figures coming down the stairs.

'Please, don't kill me,' she begged, breathless and scared. She stumbled backwards and fell down. She crawled up against the wall.

Her vision now cleared enough to see the five men. Two older men, Achilles, a man slightly older than him and a young boy, not older than fifteen. The room around her, now filled with light, revealing a ripped beige sofa pushed to the wall opposite the bed. Also, under the staircase shelves had been built in. One of the older men, approached the top shelf and picked up a thick piece of rope, just like the ones her grandfather had used to tie his boat. He nodded to the boys and together they approached her, yanking her up by the shoulders and throwing her to the bed. A cloud of dust bounced off the bare mattress.

'Please, please,' she cried. 'Achilles, why?' she sobbed. His cold expression ignoring her, scaring her.

The two boys placed her on all fours, while Achilles ripped off her dress with both hands.

'Please, don't rape me.'

'Rape you? That sounds so cold and painful. Baby tits you are going to enjoy every minute,' Pantelis, Achilles' dad, hissed into her ear. 'I say, Panayioti goes first. Being his first time and all,' he continued, addressing the rest of the group.

'Really?' the young boy's face lit up.

'Go on,' his brother encouraged him.

The freckled teen pulled his blue T-shirt over his head, unclipped his belt and dropped his shorts to the floor. He kicked off his shoes and approached the bed.

'Boxers too, son. Are you going to fuck her with your clothes on?' his father, Valentino, asked in his deep, croaky voice.

Panayioti, slightly red, pulled down his boxers, releasing his erection.

'Wow, what the hell is that? Boy is packing some big guns!' Achilles yelled, his mouth open.

'That's my boy,' Valentino commented. 'You as big as your brother?' he asked his other son, Andrea.

Andrea shook his head and joked 'our village donkey is not as big as that!'

Ecstatic, the boy jumped upon the bed; the rest of the four men each grabbing a limb of Agatha's.

Roller coaster emotions.

The phrase ran through Agatha's mind. Her nana's phrase concerning life. Yesterday's bliss so far away; light years away from this moment. The moment four beasts held her down like an animal while a fifth forced himself in her with a cry of joy. Cheered on by his family, the fifteen year old boy pounded away in pure delight. Minutes later, he asked where he should finish as if he was completing an everyday chore. Oblivious to the human being whose soul he was raping.

'Mouth, boy,' his father advised. 'Always the mouth when you're not wearing a suit. We don't need this rich bitch bearing our genes.'

Achilles grabbed her cheeks and squeezed hard, forcing her mouth to open. Panayioti stood next to her; penis in hand. The next scene took years of therapy to erase from her mind. By the time, she recovered from the shock; Andrea had forced himself in her.

'Please, stop,' she managed to beg.

'Don't worry. I'll stop. I'm not a cunt fan. I like the back door,' he said while pulling her hair back and biting into her neck, proving to Agatha he was the biggest sadist of them all.

'Turn her around, son and go for the ass so I can fuck her at the same time,' his father said. Agatha could not believe her ears. These men were ecstatically happy to have found an opportunity to live out their porn-inspired fantasies.

'What have I ever done to you? I don't deserve this...'

'You have no idea the damage your family has done to ours, you filthy piece of shit,' Achilles' dad yelled, his face turning red. That is when she noticed the naked middle-aged man with the hanging beer belly holding the video recorder.

Tears fell freely. She started to pray.

'Son, shout this bitch up, she's depressing the moment,' Panteli ordered, pressing pause on the recorder.

Achilles grabbed her face again, looking deep into her eyes. A total stranger stood before her. This was not the boy she fell in love with.

'You dare to bite me and I'll kick you to death,' he said, the coldness in his voice sent shivers down her aching spine. She reluctantly opened her mouth.

'Good girl,' he said in the same tone as he praised his Labrador.

'Wow, look at the bitch taking three cocks,' Panayioti laughed. 'I want seconds by the way.'

'Don't get greedy, boy,' his uncle Panteli said. 'Come hold the camera. I haven't had firsts yet. Besides, we will be here for three days. There will be plenty of time to fuck her whenever you want.'

Words Agatha never forgot. The moment she realized she would re-live the torment for three whole days. She prayed for salvation; even begged Christ to let her die.

She wasn't as lucky as that.

All five men had their way with her, alone, together. Every now and then, one would dash upstairs and bring down cold beers and snacks. They sat around enjoying the show as if it was the most natural thing, as if it was a summer concert or play. Agatha gave up resisting, trying to find solitude inside her mind. She questioned why they were doing this and unable to reach any logical conclusion, she let her mind drift away to happier thoughts. Days on the beach with her friends, late nights talking about boys with her sister, running in the rain, summer holidays with her parents. The grunts and the cheers of the animals cycling her diminished, the smell of their sweat vanished, the pain of them inside her was deemed insignificant, the red blood oozing from her private parts faded away. She detached herself from the horror and lost herself in blissful thoughts. Hours later, the beasts gave up for the day and retreated upstairs for showers and an outdoor barbeque. Panayioti only came down to bring her a bowl of leftovers and a bottle of warm water.

'Eat and rest. I can't wait till tomorrow,' he said, sending her kisses and imitating licking her.

The lights were switched off and shadows came out and devoured the room. Every single muscle of hers ached. The smell of sweat and bodily fluids filled the air of her confined prison. Disgusted and ashamed, she screamed and screamed until the screams turned into crying and curled up, naked, bloody and abused she fell asleep.

Agatha would swear she did not dream that night. Her mind and soul seemingly incapable of producing any dream or even a nightmare. Nothing could save her and nothing could be worse. Her body had passed out and was only awakened by the splash of icy water from Andrea's pail. Before all her senses could come alive, Andrea had already sat her up and tied her arms to the bed.

'Breakfast time, whore. You will need your strength today,' he said in his cool manner that would haunt her in years to come. 'You better behave or else,' he continued, grabbed her by the hair forcefully and smacked her hard across the face. 'Do you understand?' he raised his voice, yet never losing his cool.

She nodded, much to his delight. Panayioti approached with a plate in hand. His mischievous grin and the video camera in hand worried her. These sadists had something in mind.

Andrea opened his zipper and with his right hand he pulled out his penis. He then picked up a piece of bacon and placed it on it. 'Best spoon you'll ever have,' he chuckled. Agatha turned away, only to be grabbed again by the hair. With his other hand, Andrea grabbed her pearl earring and ripped it out of her flesh; his face revealing his delight upon hearing her screams.

'I told you to behave,' he said. 'Now, eat!'

Agatha reluctantly obeyed. Bread and eggs, followed; fed in the same manner.

'Panayioti, stop jerking off. The whole scene will be shaky,' Andrea shouted to his camera-holding brother. Panayioti giggled and pulled up his pants.

Agatha swallowed down the last piece of bread.

'Thirsty?' Andrea asked with fake kindness as he stood up and started to urinate over her face. Panayioti laughed out hysterically.

'What the...? Boy, you better wash her up and have her ready for us or you're the one going to get a beating,' the heavy voice came from up the stairs.

'Don't worry, uncle. We'll wash her right away.'

'Good,' he said and walked back up.

Andrea untied her arms. Red bruises travelled around her arms caused by the thick rope. Panayioti turned off the camera and helped his brother to pick her up. They threw her to the corner where another pail of icy water awaited her. A brown sponge floated in it.

'Wash yourself, you filthy woman. And especially your lady parts. Now!' Andrea ordered and threw her a bar of soap. Agatha trembled the entire time, yet resisted speaking. She knew it would only make matters worse. She took the soap and dipped it in the water. The bar of soap felt good as it journeyed upon her red, bruised skin.

'Quicker,' Andrea barked, like the animal he was.

Sobbing and numb, she picked up the sponge. Andrea grabbed her hand and guided it between her legs.

'Like this,' he said and scrubbed hard.

His tough, large hands were scrubbing her back when the rest of the pack came down. His long face with the small evil eyes, watching her the entire time she washed. So much hatred gathered and she had no clue why.

As she stared upon her captors in disgust, a terrifying thought spawned in her mind's darkest corners. They were surely going to kill her. She had seen their faces, heard their names; she knew everything about Achilles. Uncontrollable crying came over her and she fell to the ground on all fours.

'What a way to start today's fun,' Achilles said. 'She was always a whiner. Spoilt little brat.'

'Get up, you ungrateful bitch. And stop your crying or so help me God, I will hurt you more,' Panteli spat out, his tiny lips moving angrily, hidden in his thick white mustache. He moved towards her and snatched her by her wet, tangled hair, lifting her up.

'There is no God,' she screamed and spat in his face. Panteli stopped moving for a second. He lifted his right hand and gradually wiped away her gob from his cheek. He smiled evilly, looked around at his stunned comrades and punched her in the stomach. Agatha's petite body folded in excruciating pain.

'Tie her up,' he ordered the younger members of the group, who eagerly picked her up and flung her on the dirty bed. 'No, tie her the other way. Daddy wants some ass today.'

Agatha laid face down and watched as his heavy belt fell to the ground. He did not bother to undress. He unbuttoned his jean trousers and lowered its fly. Soon, she felt his whole body on top of her.

'I'll teach you to show some respect,' he whispered in her ear, licked her neck, then his fingers.' She struggled to move, but in vain. The ropes just dug further into her pale skin. She felt his wet fingers caress her and then, with a heavy grunt, Panteli pushed himself inside her. She held her lips tightly shut. She had decided to offer the monsters no satisfaction from watching her suffer.

Her insides, still in pain from yesterday's ordeal, burned in agony. Panteli breathed heavily as he kneeled behind her, rapidly raping her, pulling out of her and pushing himself back in. She wished he had a heart attack every time she heard him breathe with difficulty. He started to grow tired and lean on her. Unable to support the weight of the obese fifty year old, Agatha fell down into the mattress. All of Panteli was on top of her. She felt like she was suffocating, the heat unbearable. She could not keep her lips shut any longer and began to breathe and gasp for air.

'Enjoying yourself, I see,' Panteli whispered into her ear, biting down on the lobe. His breath stunk of alcohol.

'I'm going to come,' he proudly announced, signalling to Panayioti to come closer for the finale. The teen approached with the camera and zoomed in as his uncle pulled out and ejaculated over Agatha's back.

'Now, zoom in on the face,' he directed as he picked up his semen with his fingers. 'Dinner time, baby tits,' he announced. 'That's a good girl,' he said, enjoying the young girl's ordeal.

*The five men recorded the vicious rape.

Chapter 18

Tick. Tock. Tick. Agonizing tock. Seconds were flying by, gathering together and becoming minutes. My body wet and sore, my soul broken and defeated. I stumbled towards my room's en suite bathroom; clothes fell to the carpet floor as I trudged along. Boxers fell last as I slammed the door behind me.

Great. Now, even my pee is beginning to hurt. I must be coming down with something.

I flushed the toilet and in a state of daze, watched the yellowish water cycle and disappear before appearing back, pure and clean. Catharsis. I wish it was that easy with humans, too. To press a button and come back shiny and new.

Stop philosophizing, Costa, and get in the freaking shower, already. You know what it is you have to do. You have spoken enough. It is time for your gun and threats to speak.

My aching feet managed to overcome the bath tub obstacle and enter the shower. My ankles seemed to have doubled in size. I know they carry around my heavily boned body, but lately as I unwillingly approached the half century mark of my existence, I had lost weight by being careful. I still enjoyed my food, yet I cut down on the alcohol, the juices and the two spoons of sugar in each of my three daily coffees. I even finished my salad that up to my late thirties was just a decoration on my meat-filled plate. Still, my weight was no excuse for feeling this tired, this sore. I guess my emotional state did not help either.

Focus, man. Get a grip.

My hands turned on the hot water. It burned my skin as it fell and I let it. Sweat and dirt streamed down me and cycled the drain. Two minutes later, my body felt better; in contrast to my dark spirits.

I exited the bathroom naked, water still dripping down off me, blue towel in my right hand, roughly drying my thinning brown hair.

I froze at the sight of the small cardboard box lying in the center of the bed. The towel free-fell to the floor. I rushed to the box, lifting it up. It was light. I threw off the paper lid and looked inside, my heartbeat beating the record of a hummingbird.

A ball of tin foil and a piece of paper.

'I warned you, Captain, but you did not listen. You did not take my threats seriously. I promised to return your spouse in return for your silence, yet you searched for her all day. Why? To release her and then make the murders public? Have us all arrested until you find me? Well, Captain, I do not plan on getting caught. And you will DO NOTHING to stop me. If you continue, FORGET your precious TRACY! She will be returned to you piece by piece! Each time you try to find me, she will suffer. The first piece of her is in the tin foil. Remember, it's on you, not me. I warned you and you did not listen.'

My God, please, no. Tracy...

My hands picked up the ball of foil. Trembling they pulled the foil aside.

No, no, no...

I yelled like an angry animal, dropping the foil to the floor. I yelled again as my punch smashed the mirror hanging on the wall beside me.

In the room next door, Ioli turned off the flowing water. She was not sure if she had heard a scream. She squinted her eyes and turned her ear towards the wall separating our rooms. A loud smashing sound echoed through her bathroom. Shampoo still in her hair, she leapt out the tub, grabbed the biggest towel from the pile in the cherry wood cabinet and with her gun in hand rushed out into the hallway. She paused at my door, leaning closer to eavesdrop. Only silence. After two seconds of inner debating whether to knock or not, she pulled down on the handle, hoping the door was not locked.

I saw the door handle lower and quickly reached for my towel. As I wrapped it around me, blood dripped from my palms. I pulled out a tiny fragment of glass out my index finger as Ioli's gun entered the room, followed by a fully-alert police Lieutenant. Her eyes scanned the room from left to right. She realized that I was alone.

'Costa? What the fuck? What happened?' she breathlessly asked, kicking the door closed behind her. 'Is that blood?' she asked in a high pitched voice as she rushed towards me and took my hands into hers. It was then, I realized, that my hands were shaking uncontrollably. It took me a while to reply to her series of questions.

'I'm... I'm fine,' I groaned and pulled my hands out of hers. I took a couple steps back and slid down the wall. I sat on the floor

217

and pointed to the box and the ball of foil standing beside it. Her wary eyes studied me before turning and focusing on the brown, cardboard box. She knelt with caution; only a towel covered her body. I saw the shock spread over her now ashen face. She exhaled deeply and reached into the box for the note. Then, the color in her high cheekbones reappeared and a smile was born upon her face.

'Are you smiling?' I asked with amazement and curiosity coloring each word of my three word question.

'You thought this was Tracy's finger?'

I stood up. My eyes widened. 'Please tell me that is Cassandra's missing finger.'

'Of course it is. The cut is not fresh, you can see the difference in the color where the missing ring was and Tracy's nails were not shaped this way. I polished her nails red just the other day.'

I clumsily leapt forward and took her into my arms. 'Thank God. I did not even think to check the finger. I read the note first and my mind jumped to the worst conclusion...'

'Err, boss?'

'Yes?'

'You can let go, now.'

The image of the two of us standing there hugging naked, but for our towels was bordering between funny, awkward and inappropriate.

'Oh, yeah. Sorry.'

'Of course you presumed the worst. That is exactly what the killer wanted you to believe,' Ioli said. 'We have to stop searching for her, don't we? We cannot risk...'

'Go dress,' I interrupted her. 'I'm tired of playing games. We are taking charge and no one threatens us. It's our turn to act.'

Ioli placed her hands upon my bare shoulders. 'I trust you 100%.'

With a smile, I replied 'glad to hear.'

'So what's the plan?'

'We gather *everyone* in the dining room. It is time to really interrogate.'

'Give me five minutes,' she said and turned to leave.

'Oh, and Ioli?'

'Yeah, boss?'

'Don't forget your gun.'

Her smile widened. 'I never do,' she replied, lifting her armed right hand. As the door closed behind her, I turned to the window. I gazed out into the wild mayhem on going outside. The charcoal sky was blackening by the minute.

Short winter days.

My eyes grew watery. Tracy hated the winter because of this. An avid fan of the siesta, she despised the early rolling in of the night during winter months. She would always complain about how she never had enough daylight to finish all of her to-do list.

My sweet baby.

More determined than ever, I quickly dressed. Another dull pair of pants, a white shirt and my grey jacket covered my body as I mechanically dressed; my mind set on my goals, analyzing my theories. Ioli normally trusted her gut, her instincts, yet I never was one for acting upon them. Now, with Tracy's life on the line, I was ready to shoot and hope to score.

This time round, Ioli knocked upon the wooden door. I opened to find her dressed in a pair of blue jeans that flattered her silhouette, a white shirt tucked into her jeans that stood with the help of an elegant, thin, black belt. Her black high heels were on; her eyes had reached mine.

'Aren't you cold?'

'The heating is on all over the house and anyway, I feel flushed. Your eyes scare me.'

'Good. Let's hope they scare the ones I need them to,' I said and strode down the hallway.

'Aren't you telling me anything more? How am I supposed to back you up...' Ioli began to say as she quickened her pace to catch up with me.

'No time. We need to get everyone immediately into the dining room. We can't give the killer any chance of escaping, any time to get to Tracy. Besides, I fear that you might talk me out of it or say something to blow my theory out of the water and then I will be left with nothing and Tracy is still out there.'

'OK, I'll take the bedrooms and then go down to the servants,' she replied, not questioning my plan.

'And I'll take the bottom floor. Everyone into the dining room.'

Just then, the text I was expecting came from Headquarters. I avoided talking over the phone due to the cameras hidden around the house. I had texted them in the morning asking about details of a fallen plane and to validate a gossip report.

'The solution is in the details, always,' as my former partner used to say.

Chapter 19

Myriads of tourists walked up and down the beach front, the paved road of Naxos town; the fishing boats still upon the serene, turquoise waters on one side and the taverns and souvenir shops on the other. Large cruise ships stopped at a distance and deployed more sun and fun-seeking folks of all ages. The mid-day, Greek, summer sun burned strongly from above their heads and the cool sea breeze enjoyed over night had vanished, melted like a popsicle under the furious sunrays.

Further down, people searched for a place in the sun upon the sandy beach of Agios Georgios. All of the sun beds were full, a line of umbrellas shielded playing-in--the-sand young ones and tanned, fit twenty-something year olds played with their beach rackets with the clear waters reaching up to their knees, lilos floated amongst swimmers and seagulls flew above their heads. The beach bars in the center provided beverages to the thirsty people under the sun, but in vain. Naxos, famous for its nightlife, filled its tourists up with cheap beers, quality local wine and spirits for all tastes. Alcohol and heat waves do not match and will keep you thirsty for hours.

Just a ten minute drive away from all the commotion, a young girl continued to face much more serious issues than a hangover and thirst. It was the fourth day of Agatha's imprisonment. For three days, the five beastly men had raped her body and soul. Agatha had given up. She fought her captors no more. She obeyed and carried out all of their perverted requests, anything to avoid being bitten, burned, beaten or humiliated by being urinated upon again.

The silence scared her. In the beginning she was glad no one had come down this morning, then, hours later, fear took over.

Where were they?

What if they have left me here to die?

What if they are planning on how to kill me?

Questions ran freely and wild in the darkest corners of her mind. Her arms had gone numb; they remained tied up for such a long period of time. After being raped by all five men and fed their barbeque chicken leftovers, Achilles and his father, Panteli tied her up for the night. It must have been around midnight. She remembered watching the seconds go by on Valentino's black watch as he raped her. Normally, young Panayioti would come down in the morning to untie her and bring her breakfast.

Where were they?

She closed her eyes and imagined the perfect scenario. The police had arrested them in town and were searching for her. Soon, they would be at her door.

The growling of her stomach brought her back to reality. Hunger had tormented her during her stay in hell, beating out the pain she felt in her private parts, the pain from the kicks and punches, the pain from being whipped upon her back, the pain of teeth marks on her breasts, legs and ears, the pain in her soul.

She lay naked with an empty stomach and a full bladder. Tears fell from her watery eyes as she decided not to hold it any longer.

With fear of being punished, she urinated on the bed. Soaked in her own filth, she closed her eyes and tried to let her mind escape; to picture other times, other places, other faces.

More hours later, the slamming of the door above caught her attention. Heavy footsteps were heard and the rattling of the basement's door being unlocked echoed down to her below. Achilles, dressed in his green swimming trunks and a white T-shirt, came down first, followed by his father. Panteli scratched his thick beard and lit a thin cigar.

'How's my favorite whore doing today? Did you miss us?' Panteli asked in a joyful mood, blowing smoke in Agatha's direction. Agatha did not dignify his ridiculing with a reply.

'Hungry?' he continued. 'We enjoyed a feast fit for kings. Unfortunately, all good things have to come to an end, sugar tits, and we took my brother and my nephews to the airport. We have jobs and families to return to. We can't stay here all week satisfying your needs.' He could not resist laughing sadistically at his words.

Agatha's heart beat accelerated. '*This is it*,' her inner voice said. '*They are going to kill me.*'

'Where was I? Oh, yes. A feast fit for kings. We had an entire lamb, the five of us. Delicious,' Panteli rambled on as Achilles, with his new-found icy, apathetic look, approached her and started to untie her.

Her arms fell, numb and sore, to the filthy mattress. The ropes had cut into her pale skin, creating crimson rivers around her wrists. She tried rubbing them, but it only made the pain worse. Her pallid face remained calm, never showing her captors any sign of pain.

'Get up and get dressed,' Achilles ordered and threw her a pair of jeans and a pink tank top. His voice was distant and cold. Slowly, Agatha turned and brought her scarred legs to the side of the bed. She shivered as her feet touched the cement floor. Blood rushed down her veins. Her muscles twitching and aching as she struggled to pull up the jeans over her bare body; the tank top fell easily over her head. A sense of dignity was re-born as she finally covered herself. She had been naked for her entire stay in the basement.

'At least, they will find my body dressed, tossed like a piece of trash in some ditch by the road,' she thought.

'Move it. Up the stairs,' Panteli's scruffy voice barked furiously, his right hand pushing her forward.

With small, steady steps, Agatha walked towards the wooden stairs and started to ascend towards the bright sunlight beaming in from above. Weak and exhausted, she stumbled upon the fourth step and fell forward.

'Move it, bitch. We haven't got all day,' Panteli complained in the same manner you would complain about the weather. Torturing her came so naturally to him. 'Get up,' he said and pressed his lit cigar onto her shoulder. Agatha shrieked in pain, yet stood up and walked up the steps.

Reaching the top floor first, she immediately ran to the door. Locked. Her eyes looked outside the window, searching, hoping for another human being. No one was to be seen. Just dirt, dried-up bushes and stubborn olive trees.

'Get back here,' Panteli said, laughing and pulling her back by her dirty, unwashed hair. 'Sit down,' he ordered and threw her onto the old sofa, the one against the moldy wall, the one she complained about upon her arrival just before being beaten and hurled down into hell.

'Let's begin today's presentation with some history, shall we?' Panteli announced as if talking to an audience. He did not even stare at Agatha.

Achilles sat down beside her with a smirk painted across his smug face. He applauded his father and settled back into the sofa.

'Our story, children, begins *many* years ago...' Panteli began his story. He spoke for a good ten minutes. Agatha could not believe her ears. Her eyes widened and jaw lowered, leaving her mouth open for most part of Panteli's retelling of the past. All she had been through for a stupid vendetta. Crete, her beloved island and its traditions, left a sour flavor in her throat and twisted her empty stomach.

'Sweet revenge!' Panteli finished his story and flashed a dark, evil smile that ran from ear to ear.

'Get to the video, already,' Achilles complained.

'Patience, patience, please,' he replied and turned towards the dusty TV set placed on the glass table behind him.

'But what would revenge be without proof for the world to see?' Panteli asked, raising his voice and taking on his public-speaker tone.

'Drum roll,' he continued, winking towards his son. Achilles played along. Silent tears fell from Agatha's trembling eyes as Panteli pressed PLAY.

Clips of Agatha from happier times flashed across the screen. Clips from times when madly in love with Achilles, Agatha posed, smiled and flirted with the camera. Suddenly, images of her breasts appeared. The screen darkened and her name came into view. The next scenes chilled her to her core.

The beasts had montaged the footage from the recordings down below and had left only scenes where she did not fight back. The sound had been replaced by soft, erotic music and none of her pleas could be heard. She could not stand watching her naked body on TV being molested by five inhuman creeps. She coughed and threw up the liquid contents of her deprived-from-food stomach.

'I don't think she appreciates the production value of our video, dad,' Achilles said and chuckled.

Agatha wiped her mouth and looked up. Sounds of her moaning had been edited over scenes where her face was not visible.

'How do you feel now that you are a porn star?' Achilles continued with his mocking.

'Please, I beg you, turn it off,' Agatha begged.

'I guess there is no point in you watching it. You are the star. You were there. Loved your reactions, by the way. I wonder how your mother and father reacted. Oh, if only I was a fly on that wall.'

Agatha could not take her eyes off Panteli. Every muscle on her body shivered and twitched. She shook her head from side to side in denial.

'No, no. You didn't.' Her voice weak, trembling, struggling to get out.

'Oh, judging by our fine postal system, I would make an educated guess and say that they have probably already had the pleasure of witnessing their whorish, little bitch enjoying five cocks. I hope they watched it all. At the end, we concentrated all the money shots. You were superb, my dear,' Panteli replied apathetically as if talking with a neighbor about the weather.

Sounds of weeping and sobbing accompanied the once silent tears. Agatha felt the urge to throw up again, yet nothing came out. Empty stomach, empty soul. She felt hollow.

'Kill me,' she managed to whisper.

'Excuse me, dear? What was that?'

'Kill me,' she raised her voice. The words came out strong and determined.

Panteli, for once, remained silent.

'You're going to kill me anyway, aren't you?'

Panteli burst out laughing. His high pitched laughter bounced around the small room. 'Kill you? What kind of monster do you think I am? No, no baby tits. You are going home. Home, to remind your bastard father everyday how we had our way with his precious little princess. To remind him every day that we won the vendetta, that we have had our revenge! How my father –now, in heaven, bless his soul- saw his sons and grandkids take revenge for him.'

Contradicting emotions overwhelmed Agatha. She breathed heavily and tried to focus. She was going to live, yet did she want to go on? The thought of facing her parents terrified her. The way they would look at her, thinking of what they had seen.

She stared at the brown, grayish sparrow that had settled on the kitchen window sill. Her mind travelled to memories long past, memories from innocent times. She must have been eight or nine at the time, when she had found a sparrow, tweeting in pain in her back garden. Though willing to help the poor creature, it fought hard to escape the shoe box Agatha carried. She had always been stubborn. Twenty minutes later, the injured bird settled in the box.

'Let it go,' her mother advised her. 'Birds cannot live with a broken wing.'

'I will not let it be the next meal for that scruffy cat of yours!' Agatha replied and with seeds, leaves and water in her hands, she ran up the stairs and took Sweety –as she named him- to her room. Each day, after school, Agatha read to her bird and retold all the gossip from her school.

'And then Mrs Kountourou expelled him from the classroom! I struggled not to laugh out loud,' she told Sweety as she held him and bottle-fed him clean, fresh water.

Much to her mother's surprise, one fine spring day, Sweety flew from Agatha's desk all the way to her bed. Days later, Agatha, mature for her age, yet with tears in her eyes, opened her bedroom window, kissed Sweety on the head and spread her arms out. Sweety did not take off immediately. He paused. Out of fear or to say goodbye? Agatha had never settled on an answer. He stared at her for a second and then leapt out of her hands. For a moment, Agatha's heart skipped a beat. Sweety fell straight down, if only for a second or two. He, then, spread his wings and nature took its path. The wind gathered under his tiny, healed wings and raised him to the skies. Agatha watched from her window as her friend flew away, over the green meadow filled with newborn donkeys wandering and eating May's fresh grass.

If Sweety could do it, she certainly could. She had always considered herself a fighter, yet life had never sent her any real challenges. Daddy's little girl with a rich mother, she had the world at her feet. Only her polite manners saved her from being labelled spoiled.

'Here's your purse,' Achilles said, interrupting her thoughts. He threw the Gucci purse with force, hitting her in her chest. 'What are you waiting for?' he continued, raising his voice. 'Get out. Walk to town and...' He paused. He knelt beside her, his right hand grabbing her face. He squeezed her hard, hurting her. His eyes lit up with fury. '... and never speak a word to anyone about what happened here. If we ever hear from the police or anyone else for that matter, your video will be leaked and distributed all over Crete. Get it?'

Agatha nodded until Achilles let go of her. She stood up and without turning to look at either of them, she steadily walked out of the door. As she stepped outside, she quickened her pace, yet resisted running. She could feel their eyes following her down the dirt path. Her heart was about to burst out of her chest. Her mind was not able to register how she felt. Joy? Could she ever feel such an emotion again? Her mind remained blank for the next half an hour; until she reached the outskirts of the rural town of Chora.

Her legs ached, and pain vibrated her muscles. She leaned against an old olive tree next to the road. There, she collapsed in tears. Her whole body participated in her grief. She rocked back and forth, curled up under the tangled tree trunk. Flashbacks of the previous days ran through her mind. There, Agatha buried her pain, her disgust, her soul, her innocence. She let every dead part of her, ooze out of her. Determined, she finally stood up, and with her head high, she walked into town, headed straight to the port and booked a ticket for the next ship to Athens. She paid extra, booking a cabin. She was not ready to be among other people and her body was yearning for a shower; a wash better than the hose-down she received during her stay in the rapists' dungeon. She boarded the shiny under the summer sun boat and zombie-walked to her cabin. Weak and drained of energy, she struggled with turning the door key.

'Let me help you,' the young boy that worked in the souvenir department said, rushing to her aid. Agatha jumped in fear. She shivered all over as she felt his hand brush against hers.

'I'm sorry. I did not mean to startle you,' the ginger-haired boy apologized with a great islander's smile.

Agatha grabbed the key and pushed the door open. She rushed into the low ceilinged room and slammed the thin door behind her.

'Bitch,' the boy whispered from behind closed teeth and wandered off to find another girl to aid and flirt with.

Inside the clean cabin with the stale, lavender scented air, Agatha sat down on the bed, panting. Five minutes later, her breathing had relaxed and returned to its normal rates. Then, Agatha stood up, undressed slowly and avoiding the cabin's mirror, she walked into the shower. Water fell from above and cleansed her marked, filthy body. The scent of the aromatic shower gel tickled her nose. She showered for most of the journey, unwilling to leave her watery heaven. Warm water ran down her aching arms and legs, taking away the dirt and her shame.

Her hands closed off the water. She stood there, letting the very last drop fall on her. Part one of her resurrection had been completed.

Her dirty clothes were gathered into a pile on the velvet carpet. She picked them up and threw them out the cabin's only window. Soon, they floated upon strong Aegean waves, never to be seen again. Her eyes turned towards the plastic bag she had brought into the cabin with her. The clothes she had bought at the souvenir shop at the pier. A pair of jean shorts, a white T-shirt with I LOVE NAXOS written across it and a pair of black trainers, the cheap touristy kind. Unfortunately, the shop did not sell underwear, so Agatha settled for a plain, white bikini. She dressed quickly. Part two of her resurrection.

The final part took longer to complete. Back in her apartment in Athens, she packed a single suitcase. She took only memorabilia brought with her from Crete. She did not plan on taking anything else. She wished to take nothing that reminded her of Athens or Achilles. She made two phone calls. One to her landlord, coldly informing him that she was leaving, and was never to return.

'But... but why? What is wrong? Anything you need...' he rushed to say, anxious not to lose a steady income. Agatha slammed down the phone. Pointless conversations were not part of her plan.

The next call was to the airport. She was informed of the next flight to Crete, booked a ticket and without looking back, she walked out of her apartment and out onto the street. She crossed through the flow of people rushing up and down the hot, cement pavement, careful not to touch anyone. She stood on the edge, waved down the first taxi she saw and headed to the airport.

Upon the plane, she tightened her belt. For a moment, she closed her eyes and was ready to pray to God to give her the strength to face her parents. Then, she remembered. God was dead. At least he was to her.

With a rumble, the aircraft left solid ground behind and took to the skies, returning Agatha home.

Chapter 20

Night fell, along with the heavy rain. The mansion stood silent on the hill it occupied. Dark clouds surrounded it and cracked the night sky with lightning.

Inside, all of the rooms and long corridors were empty of people. All had gathered in the dining room, all were wondering why. None had been allowed to escape. A stern 'no' from either me or Ioli to any requests to go back to their rooms, to use the bathroom, to finish what they were doing at the moment; they were ordered to proceed immediately into the dining room.

Ioli and I entered the room last. Half of the guests sat around the long, dining table with the lit red candles, while the other half stood around it. The staff stood close to the wall beside them. Whispers amongst couples and friends were heard, yet no one retaliated against being dragged into the warmed by central heating room. The fire burning high in the marble fireplace was just eye candy. The room was too vast to be heated by the flames that lashed out high and crackled between the olive tree logs.

Ioli shut the door behind her and stayed there, gun in hand. I steadily walked past the crowd of people to the opposite end of the table. I stood before them, my red eyes reading each one. Several gasps were released as I placed my firearm on the wooden, cool surface of the long table with the thick legs that were engraved with imitations of Minoan designs.

'Captain, what is the meaning of all this?' Cosmas spoke first, sitting on the opposite head of the table, with Annetta's hands upon his shoulders. She denied the offering of a chair by Gianni, saying that she felt fine and stood by her broken-spirit brother.

'We are here to untangle a web of lies, Cosma.'

'Lies?' he asked, the rest of the group remaining still.

'Lies are told every day. We all tell them. We all use them. Label them. White lies, all necessary lies, right? Yet, in the innocent lies, the dark ones find room to grow. You have *all* told me and my partner lies since the very first day we arrived on this island. Some of you, I believe, are even lying to yourselves.'

'Is this leading somewhere, Captain?' Uncle Thomas asked, politely.

'It is leading to the true murderer of Cassandra, the murder of Irene Zampetaki and the abduction of my wife, Tracy!'

Now, I had them all in a stir. Some shouted how Cassandra was killed by Maria Marousaki, some about how Irene committed suicide, Anna tried to ask about Tracy and Christina asked Katerina to hold her as she felt like fainting again. As the commotion died down, I continued.

'Silence, please. I was talking about lies. Cosma? You've lied quite a lot, haven't you?'

All eyes turned towards him. He did not speak.

'Clueless about the will, huh? Two dead daughters? Cameras all over the place, huh? Did not think to mention that, did you? You could have provided us the tapes...'

'I went over all the footage!' he shouted out, interrupting me. 'I watched as my baby girl, left her room, exited the house and struggled in the rain to go to the pool house. No one else left the house and there is no camera in the pool house. Of course, if there was something to show, I would have. Irene...' He paused for a moment after saying her name '... said there was no point in revealing that we had cameras around the house. Now, I demand you tell me what did you mean by Irene's murder? Was my wife murdered?' he asked, raising his voice.

I stared at him for a moment. 'Yes.'

He swallowed with difficulty. 'Who?'

'All in good time. We are still going over the lies. Insignificant lies had to be pushed aside. Like Homer's ongoing affair with Alexandra and how he inherits Irene's money.'

Many faces turned white. Homer's parents were the most pale. The four bridesmaids breaking into a group of three and a group of only one.

'Now, that was a revelation hard to push aside. Yet, it really has nothing to do with either murder.'

'How about you finally do reveal something that has to do with the murder?' Jason asked, his young blood boiling.

'Leonida, you are adopted, right?' I asked, catching the relaxed fellow off guard. He placed his whiskey-filled glass down and stared at me.

'Yes,' he replied with a shaky voice. 'What has that got to do...'

'Which means you and George are not blood related, right?'

Neither replied.

'When was it you first fell in love? With each other, I mean.'

'My God,' Gianni said, and searched for a chair in which to sit down.

Melissa and Kallisto's eyes met in horror.

'Now, who is telling lies? What proof do you have to accuse us?'

'Not solid proof, I admit. Just your matching clothes, the way you stare at each other, the way George tells you off about drinking, how you both found *girlfriends* in the last year to accompany you to a wedding where your relatives would gather, your kisses on the stairs to the attic...'

Normally calm George, stood up and spoke louder than ever before. 'Now, listen here, you have no right...'

'Oh, but I do. Because your lie leads to the solution.'

'Bullshit. We have nothing to do with any of this,' Leonida cried.

'No, *you* don't. But your *girlfriend* does.'

'Me?' Kallisto dragged out her shriek.

'May you please approach me, dear? Sit here, for a moment.' I patted the back of the chair in front of me. Kallisto looked around at all the eyes focused on her, yet it was my trembling eyes that scared her the most. She shook off her nerves and took on her role for one last time.

'This is preposterous,' she said in her diva voice and flicked her hair back. She stood up, ironed down her dress with her hands and walked towards me. With an icy look, she stared into my eyes and reluctantly sat down.

Her bright red lipstick shone against her now ashen face. Her mouth opened slowly as she searched for the right words. I gave her no such opportunity.

'I'll do the talking. Ioli control the crowd,' I said as I lifted my gun and placed it at her right temple. Kallisto shivered and stuttered.

'Ple.. Pleassss... Please... I...'

Multiple cries came from the crowd before me. Melissa and Mark stood up in shock.

'This is madness,' Anneta yelled, her eyes opening wider than I thought possible.

'My God, he is crazy,' Leonida said, sitting back down.

'Relax, Costa,' Anna advised.

Ioli's steady voice silenced them all. 'Sit down, now. All of you. And be quiet. Next person to talk will be arrested for obstruction of justice.' Her Beretta M9 pointed towards them, leaving them no room for any questioning.

'You claim to be a successful film star, yet can you reveal the balance in your bank account?' I asked.

'My bank account? That is private information...'

I pressed the gun harder against her skin.

'I'm broke,' she whispered.

'Louder, please.'

'I'm broke.'

'Not only broke, you filed for bankruptcy, isn't that true? Investments gone sour, I read in Gossip Cop. You owe hundreds of thousands. You have six months to pay investors off before going to court.'

'What have my financial difficulties got to do...'

'It was your reason for killing Cassandra Zampetaki.'

Gasps echoed again. Cosmas stood up, his shaking hands holding on to the table.

'Admit it,' I raised my voice.

'I will admit no such thing. You are mad.'

'Want to know how mad? You know very well my wife is missing and you have no idea how far I am willing to go to get her back,' I hissed in her ear, leaning in closer to her; my gun never leaving her skin.

'Why would I kill her? I don't inherit anything. You say money is the reason...'

'Because you are going to be paid off by Cassandra's sister.'

Cosma fell back into his chair.

'Her sister is dead,' Homer called out, still glowing red from anger about my previous revelations.

'Is she now? Cosma? I checked the fallen flight you claim your daughter to be on. Another lie. No one under the name Agatha Zampetaki or Marina Spyropoulou, the name she changed it to when you sent her away to live in the States.'

Cosma had difficulty breathing. His heavy chest moved rapidly up and down. 'Please, don't tell me my sweet Agatha is behind all this.'

'I'll get to that shortly. Now, Kallisto is going to reveal where my wife is or I will be forced to stop being so nice.'

Once again, her lips separated, yet no words were produced. I was getting tired and impatient. My Tracy was missing. The storm raged outside.

Desperate times, desperate measures and all that...

Bang! I shot my gun towards the ceiling, right next to Kallisto's ear. Her whole body moved and twitched. Her words flew out, almost covered by the various screams from the throng opposite us.

'She's in the old sewage hole behind the shed. Please, don't kill me!'

'No one moves a muscle,' I called over to Ioli, as I ran for the door.

'Boss, wait. You might need help.'

I slowed down, but did not stop. 'You *have to* stay here or they will escape.'

'They?' Ioli whispered.

'No one is to leave. No one. Mark, come with me. I might need help,' I said and rushed out the room; on my way out, witnessing the slight relief on Ioli's face from hearing that Mark was not a part of 'they'.

Mark followed me without hesitation, pausing only at the entrance of the mansion to don his black raincoat. I had already leapt out into the storm and sprinted through the muddy ground towards the relic of a shed.

'Tracy,' I yelled out as I reached the back of the cottage. Panting, I searched around.

Water had reached up to Tracy's neck; her body was numb from the low temperatures. At first, she dismissed my voice as wishful thinking. At the sound of my second yelling, she began yelping out my name. By the time I knelt above the bar seal of her prison, Mark stood behind me. We both lifted the iron cap and threw it in the mud beside us. Water fell vigorously above us, as Mark said 'Grab my feet and lower me down to her.'

I held on to his legs with tears in my eyes. Tracy reached out and grabbed his hands, her soul relieved to finally being lifted out of hell.

'You came, you came. Costa...' she wept in my arms.

Inside, Ioli ignored the pleas for reason, the begging to use the toilet, the kind requests for water.

'Everybody needs to shut the fuck up and remain still,' she ordered; for the first time, Gianni did not try to discipline her vocabulary. He remained quiet, his heart burning from all the commotion and distress.

Her eyes spread wide as I re-entered the room, soaking wet and with sludge dripping from my clothes.

'Tracy?' she asked.

'She is fine. She is with Mark, by the library's fire.'

'Thank God,' Anna said.

'So, Kallisto,' I said approaching her. 'You knew where my wife was. Do not think for a moment that my finding her alive will soften me. I will shoot again. Did you murder Cassandra Zampetaki?'

'How could I? I was with Leonida. Baby, tell them.'

'That's true, I told you...'

'What you thought to be the truth. I give you that much. You mentioned how early you two went up to bed, unlike your characters. You Leonida being a drunk and all, and Kallisto being infamous for her partying. It was Kallisto who insisted that you go up to bed, wasn't it?'

Leonida nodded in reply, his eyes shaking, waiting for my next words.

'You, also mentioned how you were surprised you fell asleep so easily after having a shower, the hour being so early and how as a light sleeper, the thunder would keep you up. Spiked his drink, Kallisto?' I asked, placing the sleeping pills in front of her, which I had found in her bag while Ioli had been ordering everyone to leave their rooms and proceed to the dining room.

'Those are for me.'

'I'm sure they are. Now back to the details. You once worked as a make-up artist, right? You even bragged how great you were.'

'Yes...' she replied, her throat closing up.

'Ladies and gentlemen, there was never an aunt Myrrine. The old lady we all saw is sitting right before your eyes. Kallisto, you gave an Oscar-worthy performance, I'll give you that much.'

Silence. Shock. Letting it all sink in.

'But how?' Gianni finally spoke.

'We never saw them together, none of us. On the ferry here, Kallisto retreated to her cabin. A weird choice for an hour's trip. A cabin where Leonida fell asleep once again. A cabin where in her large trunk –in which we were all supposed to believe a diva carried clothes, shoes and accessories- she carried a wheelchair. Kallisto wore her wig, her fake skin and became Aunt Myrrine. It was as Aunt Myrrine she came with us on the bus. Leonida, you were alone in the taxi here, were you not?'

'Yes, we were going to come up here with a cab -Kallisto refused to board the bus- but at the last minute she told me to go on ahead alone with all our luggage as she wished to shop at the shops down at the bay. I saw her last in our cabin.'

'Of course. A cabin from which she once again came out of as Aunt Myrrine. Then, at the party, we all saw Kallisto, and the old lady was nowhere to be seen.'

'You have no proof,' Kallisto snorted.

'That is up to a court of law to decide. Anyway, I am sure that when the storm calms and we get a forensics team up here, they will find the murder weapon tossed somewhere around these grounds, probably find your fingerprints and DNA all over the pool house and Cassandra. You are no expert. You did not plan on police being here. Agatha probably promised you that it would be classified as a murder by Maria Marousaki. Why would police search more, right? Kallisto, you are under arrest for the murder of Cassandra

Zampetaki,' I said, took out my handcuffs and grabbed her wrists, securing her arms to the chair.

Cosmas could not take the wait any longer.

'Where is my daughter?' he cried out to Kallisto, who had begun to weep.

'In this very room, Cosma,' I replied, shocking them all once more.

Cosma stared, confused, puzzled.

'The kind girl you took so easily to. The girl you could not stop staring at during breakfast; staring at her eyes. The girl, Katerina mentioned she felt she knew the best. That is because you do know her. Agatha was in front of you the whole time. Wasn't she, Melissa?'

'God almighty,' Helena Zampetaki cried out. 'Is it you, my child?'

Cosma froze before her. Melissa stood up, unsure of her next move. I raised my gun towards her. 'Will you please remove your make-up, too? Excellent job, Kallisto, you truly are talented.'

Melissa remained still for a few seconds, before using both hands to pull off her hideous, fake scars. Skin tissue fell to the ground, leaving Agatha standing before her father.

'My baby girl,' he cried, and moved to go near her.

'Come any closer and I will strangle you,' she warned, in a spine-chilling tone.

'Settle your fond feelings, Cosma,' I spoke to the fragile man. 'She murdered your wife. Your own mother, Agatha?'

'You have no idea, Captain. No idea what I have been through...'

Chapter 21

Athens, years ago

'Scared of flying, huh?' the lanky man with the bizarre, ginger goatee asked with a grin that my mother would have described as stupid. *Wipe that stupid grin off your face* would surely make the top ten of mama Papacosta's most popular sayings.

Agatha sat uncomfortably, leaned towards the window, keeping as far as possible from the man. Airplanes did not scare her, they never had did.

'It's OK, it is only an hour's flight,' the dark-haired man continued. 'Before you know it, we will be safe and sound on the ground.' The last part of his sentence came out as if he was reading some school kid's poem, rhyming sound with ground.

'Tea or coffee?' the curvy flight attendant with the long eyelashes and the full, red lips asked, pausing at their row; her blue eyes scanning the half-asleep lady in seat A, the tall man in seat B and Agatha by the window.

'Coffee, please,' the elderly woman ordered, while yawning.

'Excuse me, may I change my seat?' Agatha spoke between the blonde lady's long yawn and her silent gasping for air.

Veronica, as her name tag revealed, kept her wide smile, though her eyes ping-ponged back and forth between Agatha and the man. 'Of course, come with me,' she said in a calm voice. Agatha stood up and squinted her eyes as she inadvertently rubbed against the man's long legs. She exhaled in relief as she reached the air hostess. 'Next to a woman, if that's possible,' she whispered to Veronica.

'How about I do you one better?' Veronica asked, flashing a full, white toothed smile. 'Follow me.'

Agatha ambled along behind the attractive lady, sensing the man's judgmental look following her.

'If he only knew...'

Agatha walked behind the leggy woman all the way to the hanging, thick blue curtain. Veronica reached out and pulled the drapes aside.

'No one normally travels first class for such a short flight. But, you seem like you need your space,' she said with her professional smile replaced by a more sincere one. 'If you need anything, don't hesitate to buzz. It's the small button by the side of your chair with the funny light bulb image stuck on it.'

'Thank you,' Agatha managed to say, holding back the tears forming around the corners of her eyes.

Veronica smiled and closed the curtain behind her as she rushed back to her coffee or tea serving duties. 'All in a day's work,' she whispered to herself, as she picked up the pot with the hot water, wore her trademark smile and mechanically asked the next row of flyers what they wished to drink.

Meanwhile, Agatha had settled down in the wider, first class seat. There, she gazed out the narrow window and got lost in thought.

She wondered if she would ever feel normal again.

'What is normal anyway?' she asked herself, then looked behind her to make sure she was alone. 'Stupid Crete and its fucking Vendettas,' she lowered her voice to a breathy whisper and gazed out her window.

She pondered if Achilles ever actually had feelings for her or if he was the world's greatest actor. She reflected on how they had met and everything they had lived through together. She imagined killing him. Killing them all. She decided straight away that she would go to the police.

'So what if the world finds out? So what if they release the video? And release it where? No company would sell it if it is an ongoing rape case. By themselves over the internet? Most people don't even have a computer at home...'

That is when Agatha realized she truly did not mind if the world saw her humiliation if it was the only way to receive justice and see the bastards that did this to her go to jail. The only person she did not wish to witness the video was her father and according to Panteli he had already seen it. Again, she felt the urge to pray and ask God that he had not seen his daughter get violated that way.

'Why? Why me?' her inner voice screamed.

'I'm trying to make sense of a senseless situation...' was her last thought; a thought interrupted by the Captain's gruff voice booming over the aircraft's built-in speakers.

'Ladies and gentlemen, this is your Captain speaking. We are about to begin our final descent to Chania airport. Currently, the weather is as it is always here in Greece, sunny and the temperature a fine 27 degrees Celsius. We have certainly enjoyed having you on board today, we hope to see you again real soon, and thanks again for flying with Olympic Airlines, voted by you as Greece's best airline for a third consecutive year.'

Agatha closed her eyes, forcing her mind to shut down.

'Stop thinking...'

She exhaled deeply as the wheels made contact with the ground. Agatha rushed to get up and go to the door first. The last thing she needed was to be surrounded, and touched by fellow passengers.

'Please remain seated, sweetie,' Veronica's voice came from behind the curtains. The air stewardess had kept an eye on her. Agatha obeyed and waited for the Captain to announce that the aircraft had come to a complete stop and it was safe to unfasten your seatbelt. Then, she dashed to the door. Veronica approached her, creating distance between her and the next passenger.

'Is everything OK, honey?'

'I'm fine,' Agatha snapped. 'Thank you,' she immediately said, with her voice going soft. 'Thank you for everything,' she continued and even forced a smile.

'Are you sure?'

'You did everything you could at the moment and provided me with solitude. Now, I have to stand on my own two feet.'

Veronica winked at her and stepped forward, towards the open door.

'Thank you for travelling with us. Wish to see you again,' she said in her professional, soothing voice and watched as the young, fragile girl alighted.

Agatha forced her mind to remain quiet as she went about the procedures from plane to exit. Expressionless, she moved with the crowd, going through customs, waiting for the metal snake to move and bring out her luggage and then exiting to the bustling road outside that was filled with cabs and buses.

Agatha scanned the drivers, opting for the grumpy looking old man with the checked cap and the short cigar. He looked like the silent type. The last thing she needed to endure was a chatty, indiscreet, Greek driver. Other than a grunt that sounded like a *hello* and a *where to*, the tall man with the scruffy-looking trousers and the filthy nails did not speak during the twenty minute drive to Chania's outskirts. He did not even turn on the radio. The silence was welcomed by them both. Having suffered horribly for the first time in her life, Agatha had a new understanding of the world. Before, she would easily have deemed the tall driver with the begging-for-a-comb greyish hair as anti-social, as poor and pathetic, as a loner in a life and much more. Now, she could not resist but think about what things could have happened during his life for him to desire silence and not care about his image.

She did not care anymore. For the first time she left the house without make-up on. Just last week, travelling without wearing brand new clothes, having her hair done and wearing lip-gloss and eye shadow would have been labelled as a crime.

As the driver whistled upon seeing her palace of a house, she took out double the amount the meter read and handed it to the man.

'Have a decent cigar and a few drinks on me. We are all coping with life,' she said and exited the green vehicle. The puzzled man took the money and through the lowered window, offered Agatha a yellow-toothed, crooked smile.

Agatha stood at the high gates of her parent's property. She gazed at the mansion in the distance for a good five minutes, before grabbing the handle and entering. She walked up to the house; her right hand taking out the keys from her pocket. She rattled the lock and pushed the heavy door open.

Miss Flora was the first to welcome her, having been startled by the opening of the door. Both Mrs and Mr Zampetaki were in the sitting room on the top floor.

'Miss Agatha? Is that you?' the maid said, her eyes running up and down Agatha's plain clothes. 'Are your parents expecting you? They did not mention anything...'

'I don't know what they expect...' Agatha mumbled, before screaming as she felt two hands grab her from behind.

'You're home!' Cassandra yelled with excitement, hugging her sister and jumping up and down. 'What you screaming for, silly? It's me. God, I've missed you. It has been soooo boring with mum and dad. Actually, you came right on time. They both have been really weird since yesterday. Mum keeps crying and dad has not spoken a word,' Cassandra chatted away, oblivious to Agatha going red and breathing heavily.

The commotion downstairs alerted her parents who sat in silence upstairs. They had yelled and cried ever since receiving what they presumed was their daughter's porn video. They had tried calling her on her apartment's phone, yet received no answer.

They both rushed to the top of the granite stairs, pausing upon witnessing their daughter, neither knowing how to react.

Agatha, also, remained still, her trembling eyes focused on her parents.

'Should I prepare...' Flora began to ask, breaking the awkward silence.

'Just get back to doing the laundry, Flora,' Irene Zampetaki snapped. 'And you, Cassandra, go clear up that pigsty of a room.

Having a maid does not excuse living like a vagrant,' she continued, her eyes not staring at either Flora or Cassandra. Both remained focused on Agatha.

'But Ma, Agatha just got home and...'

'Leave!' Irene yelled. 'Now! And don't call me *Ma*, it's peasant-like talk.'

Cassandra frowned and lowered her eyes. She tried to grab her sister's hand, but Agatha retrieved it quickly. 'It's okay, go,' Agatha managed to say with a croaky voice. Cassandra, for the first time, had trouble reading her sister. Though they had eight years between them, they had always been close. Cassandra idolized her older sister and missed her daily when she left to go study in the big city.

'Fine,' ten-year old Cassandra said and stomped out the room. Flora had already retreated to the laundry room. It was common knowledge in the household to never argue or disobey Mrs Zampetaki when she was *upset* as the older members of the staff called it. Bitchy was the word most popular among the younger members.

Cosmas and Agatha remained still, staring at each other. The silence between them was deafening. Cosma loved nothing more than his first born daughter, nothing came close. He never quite loved Cassandra the same, though he never admitted it. As for Irene, their initial fascination and romance never grew into love, at least into the love they had dreamt of. Agatha was his world. He often found himself remembering the first time he held her in his arms.

How tiny she was, the way her eyes focused on his, her fingers wrapped around his thumb. The first time she spoke, walked, laughed, ate. Now, every time he closed his eyes, he saw her with those men; pleasing them in ways that made his stomach turn.

'Dad, I...' Agatha began to say, having gathered enough emotional strength to explain the true situation.

'Shut up,' her mother coldly interrupted her. 'Not here, you stupid girl. The walls have ears. Let's go to the study, away from the staff,' she continued as she came down the stairs, avoiding eye contact with her daughter. She walked straight past her. Agatha lowered her head and followed her. It took a while for Cosma to move and join them in the study.

'Lock the door,' Irene ordered him, rolling her eyes; clearly annoyed with the two minutes he took to arrive.

Agatha approached her mother from behind. 'I know what you think, but...'

Her words were cut short by Irene's hand. Irene slapped her hard across her face. 'How dare you dishonor the family like this? We sent you to study and you.. you... you...' Irene's voice trembled more with every *you*. She could not form her thoughts into a sentence.

'You've got it all wrong,' Agatha said, her left cheek going red.

'Wrong? We saw you *fuck* around with God knows how many men!' Irene shrieked. Cosma lowered his head and wiped his eyes with the sound of the word.

'I was raped!' Agatha yelled back. 'And it's all your fault!,' she screamed towards her father. Cosma raised his head in shock, the words hitting him hard. His mind trying to register the word rape and make sense about how it was his fault.

'Raped?' he struggled to say.

'By Ioannis Marousaki's sons and grandsons. I was tied up and locked away. They raped me again and again all because of your family's stupid vendetta,' Agatha rushed to state her story. She panted and was nearly yelling out her defence. 'They edited the film and left only the scenes where it seems I am participating. The film does not show how they beat me and forced me to do it. The music on the film covers me begging them to stop. After the first few days, I had lost all will to fight back,' she continued, having lowered her voice. Her eyes journeyed back and forth from Irene to Cosma. Her father had covered his mouth and had fallen back into the burgundy armchair. Her mother remained expressionless and distant. Irene turned her back on them and slowly walked towards the closed window. She gazed outside, admiring her extravagant garden in full blossom. The sun was travelling towards the oceanic horizon and bright orange light surrounded the colorful flowers.

'How could you even believe such a video to have been my choice?' Agatha expressed her disappointment in her father. The one person who always stood by her, no matter what. 'Dad, it's me!'

Tears ran down Cosmas cheeks all the way down into his heavy mustache. He leapt out of his chair and opened his arms wide.

Agatha fell into his arms, leaning her head against his heavily breathing chest. His arms girdled her waist and Agatha relaxed, closing her eyes, safe in the arms of the only man she trusted enough to touch her.

'Well, aren't you two lovely?' Irene's sarcastic question hit them. They let go of each other and turned towards her. She leaned against the wall and stared at them both. 'And now? All good, hmm? So, Cosma, we take her back in and let them release the video? Continue living with this swinging axe above our heads? Continue as one big, happy family never knowing who has seen our daughter being ravaged by all those men?'

'Irene, she was raped,' Cosmas replied.

'Oh, and that is what we are going to have to inform everyone? Everyone we see who gives us a dirty look, we are supposed to guess he has seen it and explain ourselves. Oh, the disgrace. And who is to say that the bastards of the Marousaki family will not use it to threaten us for the rest of our lives? We know they want our winery! The vineyards!' Irene paced up and down, waving her arms in all directions as she spoke.

'And what is it you want us to do, mother?' Agatha interrupted her dramatic monologue.

'Save our family from the shame. Can you imagine your grandparents hearing about this? It would send them to their grave in a matter of hours. No, no. This can't get out. The Marousaki clan must think they have nothing on us.'

'And how is that going to happen?' Cosma asked his wife, who had stopped and was rubbing her face with her hands.

'Agatha leaves. Tonight.'

'And go where?' Agatha asked, her hands clenched in fists, her face red.

'To America. We have family there. My uncle George is a lawyer. He can arrange your papers and you will change your name and enroll at university over there. They have far better schools in the States than in Athens.'

'Do you even hear yourself? I was fucking raped, you cold hearted bitch. And you want to send me away the time I need to be here the most?' Agatha could not control herself. The rage she had suppressed to make it back home was rapidly rising to the surface.

Cosmas had fallen back into his armchair. His heart wanted to hug his daughter again, yet his mind produced thoughts about how right his wife was.

'I'm cold-hearted? I'm trying to protect the family!'

'The family or your lifestyle? All you want is to be able to continue to go to your galas with your nose up high.'

'You think I don't care? What about your sister? What life will she have in our small society? You, for that matter. You think you will ever find a husband? Or have children? They will hear whispers about their mother. Stop being selfish, Agatha. Be sensible. Many go to America or Australia and start a new exciting life.'

'And even if I do go, how will that stop the Marousakis?'

Irene exhaled deeply. 'As I said, you will change your name. We will inform everyone that you won a scholarship to study in America and after a while... we will announce you died.'

'Died? You *are* mad.'

'Like it or not, my mind is made up. With you dead, no one will threaten us. Who would release a movie with a dead girl? Also, with you dead and us in grief, the Marousakis will be satisfied with us being punished, with us being in pain. If you agree to this plan, you will have enough money each month to live a life worth living in America.'

'Just like everything in life, you are going to buy me out, buy my silence. And if I don't agree to your ludicrous plan?'

'Then we will disown you. You will get nothing and people will accept the lie as truth. That you starred in porn and we kicked you out.'

Agatha's eyes widened, shining from the tears gathered in them. 'You are a disgrace to the word mother. I will leave, but not to protect the family from shaming, but only to have the joy of never seeing you again.'

'Agatha...' her father said, standing up. Agatha walked straight past him. 'I knew she lacked a heart. I did not know you lacked the balls to stand up to her,' she said, marching to the door. 'I'll be upstairs packing. Make the arrangements.'

Chapter 22

'Raped! I was eighteen years old and they sent me away when I needed them the most!,' Agatha concluded. 'Dead to everyone who ever knew me.'

All eyes in the room were fixed on her; her tragic story finally rising to the surface.

'What did your sister ever do to you?' her aunt Anneta expressed the question on all our minds.

'Perfect little Cassandra, right? Well, your precious baby girl grew up and changed. She became more and more like Irene every day. She came to America to study and never once did she come to visit me. When I heard she was getting married, I called her and all she was worried about was mum's money. I asked if I could come to the wedding, disguised as someone else and she laughed. She warned me to stay away. She could not risk me ruining her perfect day. And she rubbed it in my face, how Irene had promised her all the family fortune; I was to receive nothing. It all seemed so unfair. I was raped, I was punished, I was sent away and she was to receive it all? That is when I came up with the plan. My revenge against my mother and to inherit what was truly mine. I knew that with Cassandra out of the way, Cosma would leave everything to me. All that I was entitled to.'

'That is why you wanted her ring, too,' Ioli said, coming closer.

'It was my great-grandmother's. I was the one that should have worn it on my wedding day.'

'So much hatred,' Helena Zampetaki said and closed her eyes, tears streaking down the crow's feet around them.

'You could have come to us for money, child. Was it really worth murdering your own blood? Why not plan revenge against the men that did it to you?' Anneta asked, sobbing as she searched for answers.

Agatha turned her cold look towards her. 'Well, I guess there's no point in concealing anything anymore.' She paused as an evil smile spread across her face, swollen from wearing the fake skin. 'I already killed them. All five of them. Burnt them alive, following in the footsteps of my arsonist ancestor.'

Cosma could not stop staring at the person that his daughter had become.

'This is why your background checks on Maria Marousaki showed no living relatives, mighty police Captain,' Agatha continued, turning towards me. 'They all died long ago. I came back to Crete the month after I was declared dead. And I waited. Waited for months before my chance appeared. All five went on a hunting trip, staying at a cabin in the mountains. The flames swallowed that wooden hut in a matter of minutes,' she announced, glowing proud; her smile never leaving her face.

'As you seem to be in a mood for revelations, would you do me the favor of explaining how exactly you managed to go upstairs to your mother, unnoticed in the few minutes you were seen going to the lavatory downstairs.'

Mark and Tracy's entrance to the room did not deter Agatha from admitting to her crimes. Not even Tracy's murderous look as she stared upon the woman who had thrown her into her underground prison.

'The old maid's stairs. They were closed off years ago, deemed unsafe. It was you, grandma, that persuaded arrogant Irene that maids could use the main stairwell and the steps were sealed off. I knocked on her door and pictured her face when I said my name. She must have leapt out of the bathtub. Well, she was always weak, it was easy to force feed her the pills.'

'Agatha Zampetaki, you are under arrest...' Ioli began as she approached with her handcuffs dangling from her left hand.

'Funny how it has been so long since I last heard my real name,' Agatha said, before whispering 'my work here is done.'

She, then, grabbed the knife, jumped onto the table and ran towards me. As she lunged off the table, knife stretched out, Ioli fired. The bullet hit Agatha's black, broken heart and blood shot out in the air. Her body fell with a loud thump upon the floor. Cosma ran to his daughter. Even after all he had heard, he still took her into his arms and as her last breath departed from her lips, he cried over the loss of yet another child.

Our silence, as we gazed at the tragic scene, was broken by Anna's scream to God.

Gianni had one hand on his right shoulder and trembled all over. The gun shot was the final blow to his frail heart. Mark rushed to him, only to regret minutes later that he was the one who had to inform the woman he loved, that her beloved father was no longer with us.

Anna sat down on the floor, held the hand of the man that stood by her through all her adult life, closed her eyes and prayed for her husband's soul to find eternal peace.

Ioli did not take it so calmly. She placed her head upon her father's chest and cried uncontrollably.

Hours passed in the house with many bodies. The storm finally weakened and moved on. The sight of the ferry approaching on the horizon, accompanied by the coastguard police, scattered solace through the mausoleum of a mansion.

We all departed the small island that day. None to ever return again.

Chapter 23

I have never been one to go to funerals; my erratic working hours always providing cover for not showing up to a friend's or relative's farewell ceremony. I am not one for closure, I guess. Death is closure enough and I witness it daily, no need to surround myself in other's grief, sorrow, regret, pain. I buried a child. My one and only child. On my knees, I saw my baby girl lowered into the ground. Since then, nothing has ever managed to shock me or bring sadness into my soul. My emotions died with Gaby. Even last year, when I buried my father, who truly was my best friend, a role model like no other, I did not turn mournful. My heart mostly went out to my mother who needed me by her side. The dead are dead, it is the living that carry the loss. Now, I felt the same way. I was there for Ioli. For that slight, short-lived, half-smile on her face as she saw me, Tracy and other friends from the police station outside of Saint Nicholaos church in Chania.

The February sky dressed appropriately for Gianni's final journey. A Greek man with values, a man who held his country, his family, and his religion close in his heart; the very organ that failed him. Mortality. Death will come for us all. You would presume that as animals with knowledge of our fate we would do a better job –or at least try- at living happy and at peace with one another. Yet, I wake up every morning to a new case of a murdered victim. Rage, anger, jealousy, madness. Welcome to planet Earth, where every day a war is going on somewhere around the globe.

'Your mind going over your life philosophy again?' Tracy whispered, pinching me on my hand to catch my attention.

'My mind hasn't stopped grumbling,' I replied, my stiff facial expression sweetened by how well she knew me.

'Let's get inside,' she said, closing up her coat. The wind circled us with its icy currents. The ocean breeze was hitting us hard, always with its ability to penetrate your clothes and your skin, and reach your bones.

Dressed in black, she held her grieving mother as they followed behind Gianni's shiny, wooden casket with the heavy, brass handles.

Anna, though clearly, deeply tormented, did not cry out like most Greek women tend to do at funerals. A weird sense of melancholy surrounded her. Her mind was probably fondly remembering dear moments with the love of her life. A religious woman with gratitude for the life God had helped her live, rather than pondering on things she never had or things she had lost.

The overweight priest with the golden-plated Bible began to say the psalms. His deep voice echoed around the high ceilinged church. People sat with the eyes focused firmly on the ground.

I remained standing in the back. Tracy slowly let go of my hand and went to light a candle. My eyes followed her for a while, until they noticed Mark standing alone by Archangel Rafael's icon. His eyes were set on Ioli. His expression revealing how much he wished to take her into his arms and whisper in her ear that everything would be okay and that he would stand by her. Greek men don't fall easily in love, but when they do, they fall into a trance. The hunter awakens and all their mind can think about is the woman of their affection.

The ceremony came to an end as the first droplets of water fell from the charcoal sky. Black umbrellas were opened and people coupled up to follow Gianni's coffin to his final resting ground. We walked past tall cypresses and dark green yews, amongst marble crucifixes with names and ages engraved into them. Children, adults, old folks. Mothers, fathers, brothers and sisters. The variety haunting, provoking the mind. Lives cut short at any moment. I remembered my doctor's appointment next Monday. My stomach, knee, and back pains were getting worse. Tracy finally had enough of my man-whining and booked me an appointment to have a full check-up.

Ahead, next to Ioli's grandmother's grave, a deep hole awaited us with a hill of freshly dug up dirt to its side.

The elderly priest opened his Bible and with one eye on the page and one on the approaching dark clouds, read his words in a hurry. Anna knelt by the six-foot hole and with Ioli's hand on her shoulder, watched her husband lowered into the ground. Her lips moved – maybe a final goodbye, I thought, maybe one last *I love you*- as she threw in a handful of dirt. Ioli knelt beside her, her black dress collecting mud, and threw in a handful of dirt, too. Her words, *bye my sweet, sweet daddy* were more audible than her mother's.

With a loud bang from above, the darkened clouds collided and fat droplets of water fell from the sky. Ioli's cousins took the wooden handled shovels and with sleeves rolled-up, began to fill in the grave.

Tracy approached Ioli, placed a gentle kiss on her cheek and whispered in her ear. 'Anything, anytime. Just call us.'

Ioli stroked Tracy's hand and whispered 'thanks.' In a matter of minutes the crowd of a hundred had dispersed back to the dry environment of their cars. As Tracy and I walked back to our vehicle, I noticed Mark standing under a towering oak tree, his eyes on Ioli.

'Go ahead,' I said to Tracy and ran up to meet Mark.

'You should go talk to her,' I advised, pulling him out of his daze.

'Oh, Captain. I did not see you there. No, it's not the right time. She is clearly in pain.'

'And that is when they need us the most. Come round the family's house. Everyone is heading over there for a nice, hot, strong coffee and to show our support to the family. She would love to see you.'

'Would she?'

'She wouldn't have been showing your text messages to Tracy and talking about you if she wasn't interested.'

'She only replied to one of my messages. A simple thank you to my condolences.'

'She's not a girl of texts and fancy words. A strong woman like her needs a man of action. And that is as far as my matchmaking skills go. It's up to you, Mark to be the hunter she needs,' I said and did not stay for a reply. I dashed out into the rain and ran to catch up with Tracy; my back aching every step of the way.

At least, my mission was successful. Mark did show up at the house and even in the gloomy atmosphere, he managed to make Ioli's eyes shine. After all, life is for the living and the living need to keep going on.

As for me, my mind over analyzed my doctor's appointment tomorrow morning.

'All you are going to do is let the doctor have a look at you, take your pressure and a blood sample. Stop worrying,' Tracy said, rolling her eyes, annoyed that I was not listening to a word she was saying.

She was right. The doctor listened to problems, asked a few routine questions, ignored my google-based questions, took my pressure and had the nurse take a blood sample. What Tracy did not guess was the urine test. I was given a small, plastic cup and shown to the bathroom. It's funny how when you really *have to go* you never do. I stood there, with my piston in my hand for a good three minutes before release came.

In a matter of twenty minutes, I was out of the chlorine-smelling clinic and back in my dirty car. My mind journeyed to the barbeque-flavored spare ribs I was going to order. Friday night still remained date night for us. And date night always meant eating out. The juicy meat, the aged whiskey and Tracy's fine love-making skills erased the whole appointment from my mind. Until, four days later, the phone rang from the doctor's office and I found myself over-thinking things again.

The following day, I entered through the hospital's glass doors and headed to the second floor.

I hate hospital chairs. Always cold, always hostile to your back. Even in a prime private hospital, like the one I sat in. The oversized clock opposite me, informed me that my appointment was supposed to occur twenty minutes ago.

'Take a seat and the doctor will see you shortly,' the blonde, young girl with the soothing voice had apprised me from behind her modern looking booth.

Your results are in Mr Papacosta. When are you available to visit? The doctor advises you to come as soon as possible.

That is what she had said in the same voice, with the same tone. I admit, I panicked. *As soon as possible.* That is what you would say if something was wrong.

My foot tapped upon the cold, shiny floor. My fingers fought around with each other.

Six other people sat around me.

A blonde pregnant lady had sunk back into the white leather couch outside her doctor's office. Judging by the size of her tummy, I guessed she was due any week now. Her husband sat patiently besides her wearing a hipster checked shirt, a sports cap, a thick black beard and a worried expression.

First child, I thought before producing thoughts of jealously. *Why couldn't my pathologist have nice, comfortable sofas?*

An elderly gentleman to my left did not seem to mind the cold, hard chair. He kept nodding off to sleep. I feared to think how long he had been waiting outside his doctor's office.

Opposite me, a young woman in her early thirties, dressed in a flowery dress fought hard to keep her two boys busy. Her ammo in the war against boredom included coloring books, toy cars, story books and action figures. All failed. Her green eyed twins with their snotty noses only settled down when provided with their mother's phone and tablet.

'Candy crush,' they cheered in sheer excitement.

I smiled at the frustrated woman.

'Boys and their toys,' she said and proceeded to pick up after their mess.

I gazed up towards the towering clock. The hands seemed to move slower than usual. Tracy was right. I am such a bad *waiter*. Thankfully –for me- she had to work. She said she would take the day off, but I persuaded her otherwise. I love her, but there is no need to have someone next to you telling you to relax every two minutes. That only makes me nervous.

I'll relax when I want to relax.

And with that thought, the doctor's door opened.

'Mr Papacosta, the doctor will see you now.'

With sweaty palms wrapped around the chair's cool, metal arms, I lifted myself up and bee-lined behind the youthful nurse to the doctor's grey door. She held the thick door open and patiently waited for me to enter the spacious and well-lit office.

'Good morning, Costa. Please, take a seat,' Dr. Ntia Germanou said, exiting her examination room, her olive skin in contrast with her shiny, white coat. She pointed to the much more comfortable armchair in front of her wooden desk with the disc shaped, brass pull knobs. The normally-joyful doctor who loved to talk about the weather and always asked me about murder cases while laughing and explaining how she was not a psycho, but enjoyed a good mystery tale, walked past me in silence. She remained distant as she informed her nurse that she would not be needing her for this and she would buzz her when she was ready to accept her next appointment. With the nurse gone, Dr. Ntia released her tied-up, black, silky hair and let it fall to her shoulders. She settled down in her high backed chair and reached for her red glasses. She lifted the brown envelope with my name labelled on it and pulled out a few papers. Next to her was my file. Her eyes were fixed on it as if reading, yet her eye pupils revealed otherwise.

'Costa, you are a straight forward kind of guy, so I am going to be straight with you. Your tests are quite worrying. I am going to order a series of tests that I wish to be done ASAP...'

'What is it you suspect?'

'Cancer.'

Many long, fancy words came out of her mouth after the c-word. Medical terms, various procedures such as a CT scan and an endoscopy, and jokes as 'don't worry'. My mind probably did not hear half of it. It shut down the outside world and processed the one word that did stick. Cancer.

Mixed emotions overwhelmed me.

After Gaby's murder, Tracy and I fell apart. We eventually broke up and I resigned from my detective's job in New York. Days later, I decided I did not wish to go on living. However, I was not one to pity myself enough to commit suicide. I wanted to go out my way. I came back to my homeland and joined the force here, only to discover that when you remove the fear of dying from a police officer, you have your perfect crime fighter. I took on every case labelled dangerous. The dragon-rapist, the Olympus Killer, crazy monks, the Athen's arsonist, the July the 11th terrorist group, the campus murderer, the spiderweb shrink, you name it. My life was always on the line. Now, with Ioli's friendship, my reconnection to

Tracy and my acceptance –if there is such a thing- of my daughter's death, I realized that I was not ready to depart the world of the living. But, I guess, cancer would be the judge of that.

'Costa,' Dr. Ntia said, raising her voice to grab my drifting away attention. 'I realize this is a scary situation, but nothing is for sure yet and I promise you I will be with you every step of the way...'

I still remember that line of hers. 'Nothing is for sure yet...' It played through my mind during our next subsequent meeting when she announced that I had gastric cancer. Yes, my stomach -after years of being treated like a king by me, had betrayed me. Stomach cancer. Two words. Terrifying words yet for some bizarre reason, funny to me. Of all the places I could get cancer, I got it in the stomach. Two words, forcing me to regret the twenty five years of my life that I spent as a smoker, the last ten years of my life that I never spent inside a gym and the fifty years that I spent as a food lover. Oh, did I enjoy food. As Dr. Ntia put it, 'the top three reasons are smoking, being overweight and a diet high in salty, pickled, and smoked food.' Even as she listed the types of food, my mind thought of certain delicious goodies and the saliva increased in my mouth.

I drove home in silence, that day. No popular hits blurring from my aging, crackling car speakers and me singing along off key. Just me and my thoughts. One question overshadowing all other thoughts. *What the hell, I am supposed to tell Tracy?*

The sun hid behind the line of apartment blocks to my right and the darkness grew stronger. By the time I reached home, I had switched on my Audi's lights and opened the car window, letting the soft, cool night breeze caress my slightly sweaty-from-anxiety body. My cancer-cell-carrying body. An enemy from within. Your own body ganging up against you.

I parked outside the house, noticing the light from our living room TV playfully coloring our thin curtains, and unwillingly approached our doorstep. It took me a minute or two to focus enough to land the key into place and I pushed open the dark brown, aluminium door.

'Honey, you back?' Tracy called out.

'Yeah, babes,' I said, trying to paint the words with my usual happy tone.

Yesterday's terrorist attacks were playing on the television and multiple windows were open, all filled with experts analyzing the reasons why they had happened. As if that would bring back the dead. Prevention is what is needed, not an after-analysis, if you asked me.

'I can't believe what I am hearing. There is so much hatred in the world. People are over-generalizing and blaming all Muslims for this. How can you blame an entire religion?' Tracy grumbled. 'Christians blaming Islam for promoting violence. As if Christianity is so innocent! Have you read the Bible...? Ancient Egypt, Sodoma and Gomorrah, the flood, gays, witches, bastards, adulterers... all violently dealt with. Then, Christianity crusaded against the Middle East leading to Islam fighting back. Every action has an opposite reaction; all religious books are out of date. You can't blame a whole religion for a bunch of terrorists that follow the Quran literally. A lot of people followed the Bible literally and they burned women at the stakes; was all Christianity to blame? All religions have murdered millions. Whatever does not unite us, separates us. Organized religion has been a plague on the planet for thousands of years....'

Tracy's rant came to abrupt end after witnessing the wide smile on my face.

'What?' she asked. 'What you grinning about?'

'You. Your lawyer ways. I love it when you get all fired up about something.'

'Do you, now?' she said, smiling back. 'Come sit down, tell me how did your doctor's appointment go?' she continued, picking up the remote control and pressing MUTE.

I had not revealed Dr. Ntia's suspicions to Tracy. I left her in the dark. Tracy hoped the doctor would recommend a healthier way of living and prescribe me some vitamins.

'I have cancer,' I said, remaining standing. I was never one for being subtle or taking the long way to the point.

Tracy struggled to form her next words. Her smile dropped and her eyelids moved rapidly as her brain processed what I had said. A mixture of shock, disbelief and sorrow overtook her.

'Costa, if you think this is even funny, I swear to God you will be Ioli's next murder case!'

'Oh, boy,' I said, exhaling. I approached our leather couch and sat beside her. I took her hands into mine. 'I had all sorts of tests done this week. I did not want to worry you, just in case it was nothing...'

Tracy shook her head. 'What did the doctor say?'

'Stomach cancer. Well, you know Dr. Ntia. She is always optimistic. She blabbed about surgery, chemotherapy and how targeted drugs work miracles nowadays.'

Tracy stood up. 'I... I can't even hear the words.' She placed her hands on her head and walked into the kitchen. The loud smashing sound that followed informed me that the vase with the fresh sunflowers was no more. I knew my wife. I gave her time. I even read the news running along at the bottom of the TV. Commercials had to come on, for me to finally rise from the soft sofa and drag myself to the kitchen. Tracy stood with watery eyes and a cool glass of white wine. Judging by the bottle to her right, it was not her first glass. Her victim lay in pieces by the fridge, the dying sunflowers among the small puddles of water. She let the glass down slowly and walked towards me. She paused for a second about a foot away from me, staring into my eyes. Then, she fell into my arms, kissed my neck and whispered 'another thing we will face together. Don't you dare shut me out again. This is our battle, and the Papacostas play to win.'

Our next kiss was on the lips. Two fifty-year olds sharing a teenage kiss, defying danger. My fingers got lost in her curly hair as I held her close. A tender kiss, our first step in an uphill journey.

Chapter 24

Spring time in Greece is a delightful period; if winter decides to leave by March and summer does not invade in May. More sunlight hours to enjoy the beauty around you and the perfect weather in which to do so.

Not that I got to enjoy any of it. I was 'forced' by Tracy, the police Chief, Ioli and my doctors to take a six month leave from work.

'Isn't *will-to-live* a major booster for cancer patients?' I tried to trick my doctor to letting me stay at work.

'We do not live to work, Mr Papacosta. Let's beat this first and you will be back at work next year.'

'Next year?' I asked, my voice revealing the horror inside. 'Why don't you just shoot me now and get this over and done with?'

'Costa!' Tracy said, and by the look on her face she needed to say no more. Every husband knows when the last word has been spoken. I screwed up my face in retaliation and got lost in my thoughts, once again.

I am never going to go back to work...

The thought sent shivers down my spine and my bottom lip trembled.

This is not how I wanted things to end. We humans have knowledge of our mortality, but we always remained optimistic that we will have enough time. Enough time to do and say everything in our life plan. Determination came over me.

Cancer will not have the best of Costa Papacosta! I will beat your ass and be back at work as soon as possible.

My inner fighter sounded so sure of himself until my pessimistic voice replied.

Yes, you will beat cancer.

Your fifty-year old sorry ass and your hanging-from-unhealthy-foods beer belly will beat cancer.

You! With your aching back and stressed out knees. What a joke.

Four weeks later

In the evening, I sat in front of the TV flicking through the hell known as prime time programming. In the morning, I had my usual trip to the hospital for another round of chemotherapy. I had so far completed my first month of therapy.

'Utter rubbish,' I muttered.

'Read a book, dear,' Tracy called out from the kitchen; her supersonic ears able to hear me whine from miles away. She was busy preparing my favorite meal. Octopus cooked with red wine.

'Anyway, Ioli will be over shortly,' she continued.

'I thought I heard you conspiring against me over the phone.'

'Nonsense. We have better things to talk about than you.'

She did have a point. Ever since Ioli and Mark went on their first date in February, Tracy called her daily to chat about all the juicy – as she referred to it- news. I was happy for Ioli. Plain as that. And even better, if I could survive a night of gossip with my two favorite ladies, maybe I could discuss a few cases with her. So far, whenever I spoke about work with Ioli, all she would do was complain about the idiot –according to her- rookie that the Chief assigned to her as my temporary replacement. The kid was probably not as bad as she described him.

'I don't like his stupid ways, his stupid voice, his awful cologne and that dumb expression he wears every time I talk with him!'

I knew she was harsh with him, because she missed me. And worst, she feared I was not coming back. Not that she would ever admit such a thing to me. Besides, it was better than in the beginning when she would just stare at me with watery eyes and act tough, so I played along.

'What did that dumb-ass do now?' One question strong enough to have Ioli ranting for an hour.

There was no need for the mighty question tonight as the night focused on Mark. I dived into my delicious, soft, well-marinated octopus, glad that chemotherapy did not mess with my appetite as I had been warned it might. It took my first hairs last week, it put a dent in my sex life, it had every bone in my body feeling weak, but it did not take this. My appetite and love for food conquered cancer.

'I often feel like the ice queen. Mark is in love and he shows it all the time. It's too fast for me,' Ioli replied to Tracy's inquiries.

'You don't feel the same?'

'That's the thing. I do. It's crazy. I've never been the head-over-heels kind of girl.'

'That's how it is when you meet the one,' I said, leaning towards Tracy; octopus sauce dripping from my lips.

Tracy kissed me on the neck and said 'Well, what do you know? He *is* listening.'

'Nothing wrong with letting love in, sweetie,' Tracy continued, turning to Ioli.

'Yes. So let it in and let's move on to our next topic. How's the murdering nun case coming along?' I asked, causing both ladies to laugh.

'Forty-two minutes, I win,' Ioli proudly announced.

'I really believed he would last at least an hour this time,' Tracy replied.

'You two bet how long I would last before asking about a case?'

'That's right. And I won. Tracy's paying the hair salon tomorrow!'

I shook my head and lifted another octopus leg to my mouth.

'Well, you had your laugh. Now, tell me about the position in which you found the latest victim? The papers did not reveal any details.'

'Yes, I know. I have the rookie talk to the reporters. He doesn't know shit anyway, so what can he reveal?'

I threw my head back and laughed. It had been a while. 'You're so mean.'

Two months later

Even the weather felt pity for me. May came and the weather remained sweet. No sudden heat waves that had me cursing from the morning. A big guy like me sweats a lot and the heat and I have never been friends.

Outside, trees and flowers came alive in the smoky city of Athens, painting the grey and dull surroundings with multiple colors. Inside, I waited for Tracy to set off for work. As soon as she left, I ran to the bathroom and puked out my guts. Same routine every morning. I fought hard not to reveal how bad I felt in front of her. I saw no reason in bringing her down. Depression was the last thing needed right now in our household.

That is when the telephone rang. Ioli's name appeared across my coruscating green screen.

'Hey.'

'Hey yourself. How are you feeling today, Cap?'

She always asked. Always awkwardly. Her tone never like before. I hated the question, yet provided an answer. A lie, but still an answer. I guess she could not bare not to ask. She worried daily. That's the worse thing with cancer. Not the pity from people you know, but the worry you burden on the ones who love you.

'Fine. Strong as an ox.'

'Great. Listen, I'm in your area, mind if I pop round for a bit?'

I looked up and gazed into the living room mirror that hung above Tracy's so-called ornament-table. An oval, dark brown table filled with pint size souvenirs and gifts; sacred happy memories scattered over decades. My image shown opposite me, distorted compared to my memory. A thin, pale face with thinning, once pitch-black hair. Even my chest hair had began its journey to shades of grey. Below, a well-fed belly on the retreat. As I stood in my black boxers, I was sure I had the first signs of stretch marks.

'Costa?'

'Em, yeah. Sure. I will be waiting for you.'

'If it's a bad time...'

'Nonsense...'

Her cheerful laughter echoed in my ears. I used nonsense quite often. Ioli considered it a *grandma's word*. Ioli, on the other side, had a rich vocabulary when it came to synonyms for nonsense. None that I could utter around my mother and still avoid a slap on the back of my head.

'Great. See you in five.'

I threw my phone on the I-take-up-all-your-living-room sofa and rushed to the bedroom as fast as my frail knees allowed me. I dressed with my mind contemplating the fact that my mother was thousands of miles away, in New York, oblivious of her son's cancer. After losing her husband last year, she was not ready to hear this.

My finger played around with my shoe laces as I heard Ioli's red convertible drive up my driveway, Adele's latest record on full blast. She turned the volume high to be able to sing along; out of tune, pitchy, skipping words or worse, replacing them with her own, yet she still sang her heart out.

I swung the front door open before her finger reached the bell. She smiled, kissed me on the cheek and ballet danced into the room.

'Well, well, well. Someone is in high moods today.'

'I'm gonna be all girlie for a minute. Please forgive me,' she said, stretched out her arm and flashed a diamond ring in my face. My eyes stretched open like never before.

'Mark proposed?'

'Last night!'

My arms opened wide and I took her into my arms. 'I'm so happy for you,' I said, being a Greek man and holding back my tears of joy. Ioli did not manage to hold them so well.

'Minute's up,' she said, wiping her eyes and rushing to the sofa to sit down. She patted the seat next to her, calling me to sit.

As I sat down, she took my hands into hers.

'I'm not one to provide an intro to everything. My father's dead. Thus, you are the closest, living man to me. Boss, it would be my pleasure to have you walk me down the aisle.'

The proposal took me by surprise. The tears formed and a couple snake-lined down my cheek.

'God does work in mysterious ways. You lost your father. I lost my daughter. I could think of nothing I would love to do more than to give you away.'

She wiped her tears and chuckled. 'Give me away? You make me sound like a piece of meat!'

'A fine, prized piece. That doctor better take care of you...'

'Don't worry. I'll shoot his balls off if he hurts me.'

'Please tell me you did not tell him that.'

'Of course I did. This is me we are talking about.'

Laughter mixed with tears. Life's best cocktail.

'So, when's the wedding?' I finally asked, departing from our long embrace.

'August.'

'August?' the question came out in glorious shock and in high pitch. 'In the heat?'

'I told Mark you would say something about the heat...'

'And so soon?'

'I'm not going for a Greek wedding. Well, at least in the sense of running around for over a year picking dresses, flowers and deserts. And then inviting every single person I have ever met. Mark and I both agree on keeping it small. Beautiful, but small. A close few, a nice island, a sunset, a bit of dancing and of course...'

'Food!'

'You know me well,' she said with a full-toothed, long smile.

Her smile shortened and her lips met as she saw the change in my expression.

'Why the sad eyes?'

'Are you having the wedding in such a short time because of me?'

Her usual shoulder nudge hit me; more like a punch this time.

'Fuck off. Of course not. You're not on death's roll. You could give me away next year if I wanted.'

'Shall I guess the island?' I changed the sore subject, having received the reply I wanted. No need in reading more into it. She would never admit it was for me, so I lived the lie with her.

'Go on.'

'Santorini.'

'Am I so predictable?'

'Only on matters of food and islands.'

August - Santorini

If there ever was a sign of a Creator out there, it is Santorini's sunset. The majestic, turquoise Aegean waters ran for miles to the horizon to meet the clear, blue sky. Between them, the bright, blazing Greek sun in all its glory. And insignificant, little *'you'* enjoying it all from Santorini's 300 meter high, steep, rocky cliff; hanging above the caldera from Saint Gerasimo's church.

The clock struck eleven and I anxiously paced up and down outside the blue and white church, sweating even in the shade provided by the towering, ancient olive trees that outdated the church and all surrounding buildings. Inside, Tracy and other guests –no more than thirty people in total- were cooled down by the four air-conditioners working overtime on full blast. Only Mark felt the heat, though from the inside, as he waited for Ioli to arrive.

The demon of the Greek islands, also known as a heat wave, unleashed its powers and the temperature had reached one hundred degrees Fahrenheit and it was not even noon, yet. Sweat poured out of my every cell, running down my naked scalp and down to my eyebrows. I had decided on shaving off all my remaining hair for the wedding. Make myself a bit more presentable. I paused, sure of the incoming noise from the distance. I leaned on my walking cane, an evil necessity due to my weak knees and back that only got worse with my on-going sessions of chemotherapy. My image brought me to tears in the morning. I stood in front of my hotel room's mirror and witnessed a shadow of my former self. A weakling, a sick body. Pathetic, self pitying thoughts that were thankfully shot down by Tracy's warm embrace and cool kiss to my neck.

'You are still every bit of the man I first fell in love with. Now, get dressed quickly. Ioli wants me to go to the church early to make sure that –her words- idiot looking florist with the fucked up hair got everything right,' she said, and passed me a much needed frappe.

The honking coming from the approaching cars hauled me out of yet another day dream. The white Mercedes turned into the church followed by three more washed and polished cars. All sparkling under the radiant sun. Familiar faces appeared from the line of vehicles. Ioli's joyful uncle Thomas, her aunt Georgia and a large group of underage cousins dressed in white, carrying hay baskets filled with rose petals. From the bride's car, first exited her childhood best friend and partner in crime, Polina, in a dazzling peach dress with a cut running up her leg to the very top. Then, Ioli's mother, Anna, appeared dressed in black as every widow in Greece, yet an elegant dress with sewed-in details around the edges. She looked younger, despite her troubles and worries; a gift from Ioli's make-up artist and hairdresser.

All faded to the background when the bride appeared. Ioli, the tom-boy, never fond of dresses and 'girlie-things' as she referred to bags and jewelry, always with subtle makeup and her black hair in a high ponytail, stepped out of the car and stood in the sun. A magnificent, fresh snow white dress caressed her body. Silver high heels added to her height and platinum earrings fell from her ears. A dazzling necklace hung around her neck and her hair was airbrushed to heights never seen before. The glitter in her black hair playfully reflected the bright sunrays as she turned in my direction and flashed a smile with her full red lips. Color highlighted her high cheekbones and gave her eyes a glamorous look.

'You look stunning,' I managed to say, as she rushed towards me and grabbed me by the arm.

'Not so bad yourself,' she said and pulled me. 'I promised not to be late. Oh, well...'

The children entered first through the thick, wooden door, scattering petals along the ruby carpet. Ioli and I entered next, followed by her mother and relatives. All eyes turned and smiles were born all around. The largest one on Mark's face. His heart racing in anticipation as Ioli took small steps towards the altar.

Soon their hands and eyes met. Half an hour of praying, Isaiah's ceremonial dance and drinking of communion followed. The ceremony was sealed with a kiss.

I watched my partner at her merriest and wished her every possible happiness. Childless and cancer riddled, I had full knowledge of how tremendously short life could be.

One day we will all die, but on all other days we will not. Life goes on and new steps appear along the way. A battle with a disease from within, a marriage, a new case, a newborn child, a change in career... New steps.

The future unknown...

The end.

About the author:

Luke Christodoulou is an author, a poet and an English teacher (MA Applied Linguistics - University of Birmingham). He is, also, a coffee-movie-book-Nutella lover.

His first book, THE OLYMPUS KILLER (#1 Bestseller - Thrillers), was released in April, 2014. The book was voted Book Of The Month for May on Goodreads (Psychological Thrillers). The book continued to be a fan favorite on Goodreads and was voted BOTM for June in the group Nothing Better Than Reading. In October, it was BOTM in the group Ebook MIner, proving it was one of the most talked-about thrillers of 2014.

The second stand-alone thriller from the series, THE CHURCH MURDERS, was released April, 2015 to widespread critical and fan acclaim. The Church Murders became a bestseller in its categories throughout the summer and was nominated as Book Of The Month in three different Goodreads groups.

DEATH OF A BRIDE was the third Greek Island Mystery to be released. Released in April, 2016 it followed in the footsteps of its successful predecessors. From its first week in release it hit the number one spot for books set in Greece. It was BOTM in the group Mysteries and Crime thrillers and chosen as one of the best mysteries for 2016 by ReadFreely.

MURDER ON DISPLAY came out in January, 2017 and enriched the series.

Luke Christodoulou has also ventured into children's book land and released 24 MODERNIZED AESOP FABLES, retelling old stories with new elements and settings. The book, also, features sections for parents, which include discussions, questions, games and activities.

He is currently working on the fifth book of his planned Greek Island Mysteries book series.

He resides in Limassol, Cyprus with his loving wife, his chatty daughter and his crazy son.

Hobbies include travelling the Greek Islands discovering new food and possible murder sites for his stories. He, also, enjoys telling people that 'he kills people for a living'.

Find out more and keep in touch:

https://twitter.com/ @OlympusKiller

https://www.facebook.com/pages/Greek-Island-Mysteries/712190782134816

http://greekislandmysteries.webs.com/ (Subscribe and receive notice when the next book in the series is released)

Feel free to add me:

https://www.facebook.com/luke.christodoulouauthor

Note to readers:

First of all, thank you for choosing my book for your leisure.

If you enjoyed the book (and I hope you have), please help spread the word. You know the way! A review and a five star rating goes a long way (hint hint).

For any errors you may have noticed or questions about the story, let me know: christodoulouluke@gmail.com and they will be fixed on the spot! Also, email me to be added to my mailing list (2-3 newsletters yearly).

Printed in Great Britain
by Amazon